APE EARS AND BEAKY

NANCY J. HOPPER says, "I had a lot of fun writing APE EARS AND BEAKY, partly because of the situations Scott and Beaky found themselves in and partly because I like dealing with suspense, which plays an important part in the story."

Mrs. Hopper, a former teacher and the mother of two, lives in Alliance, Ohio, with her husband, a college art professor.

APE EARS AND BEAKY

NANCY J. HOPPER

AN AVON CAMELOT BOOK

AVON BOOKS
A division of
The Hearst Corporation
1790 Broadway
New York, New York 10019

The E.P. Dutton edition contains the following Library of Congress Cataloging in Publication Data:

Hopper, Nancy J.
   Ape Ears and Beaky.

   Summary: Thirteen-year-old Scott struggles to learn to control his temper, but not before it's led to all sorts of trouble, including dismissal from one baseball team, humiliation on another, and involvement with his enemy, Beaky, in a plan to catch some professional thieves.

   1. Children's stories, American. [1. Anger—Fiction. 2. Baseball—Fiction. 3. Burglary—Fiction] I. Title.
PZ7.H7792Ap   1984   [Fic]   84-8039

First Camelot Printing: February 1987

CAMELOT TRADEMARK REG. U.S. PAT. OFF. AND IN OTHER COUNTRIES, MARCA REGISTRADA, HECHO EN U.S.A.

Printed in the U.S.A.

OPM   10 9 8 7 6 5 4 3 2 1

to Patty

I should like to express my gratitude to

Dr. Stephen R. Kramer for his advice
on the counseling chapters

and

Dr. G. David Gentry for his rats.

1

The last place I ever expected to find myself in the middle of the night was at Beaky Norton's house, throwing stones up at his window. At least I thought it was his. He didn't have any brothers or sisters, and I doubted that his parents' bedroom window had one of those little signs to let firemen know there is a kid inside.

"Come on, you jerk," I muttered, my breath steaming on the cold air. "Open the stupid window and poke your stupid head out." I was so cold, but I stopped shivering when I thought about all the rotten things that had happened to me that day. I was determined to make *somebody* pay, and Norton was that somebody.

My latest troubles had started only seven hours before, when I was innocently walking with my best friend, Shawn Davis, over to the Front Street Field to ball practice. We were a half hour early. It was cutoff day for Rutledge Rims, so the extra practice with Butch and Terry couldn't help much, but it was better than waiting at home with a lump of ice in my stomach from suspense and my bratty little sister, Tina, pestering me.

There were only three other kids at the field. Two of them were way over at one end near the goalposts, practicing catch. The other was Beaky Norton.

"Not him," I said in disgust to Shawn. "Pretend you don't see him," I added, turning my back on Beaky, but not until I'd noticed his new catcher's mitt.

Beaky always has the best equipment no matter what sport he goes out for. He even has a professional-level tackling dummy for football although he is the frailest kid I know. It must have cost a fortune, and I would have lent him Tina for free.

"Look at that mitt," I said. "I bet they bought him a catcher's mask too, but it wouldn't fit over that nose." On anyone, his nose would look enormous, but Beaky is so tall and skinny that it looks like the front end of a jumbo jet sticking out of the side of a cliff.

"I think his parents should save their money and buy him an operation to make him look more like other people," said Shawn.

"Yeah, and then they could send him to some kind of camp that specializes in fattening kids up."

We both fell silent, speculating on the disaster called Beaky.

"Maybe his parents think he's okay the way he is," ventured Shawn. He pulled a long blade of grass and nibbled on the tender end. I would never do that. I have seen too many dogs around the field.

2

"I don't know," I said. "I've met his mother, and she could see all right. Maybe they already took him to a plastic surgeon, and he turned Beaky down because the challenge was too great."

"With a nose like that, you'd think he'd go out for cross-country. His lungs would never run out of air."

I didn't answer. I was remembering that I had had gym class with Beaky last year. His legs in shorts were enough to scare small children. They looked a lot like overcooked spaghetti, only they were covered with black curly hairs.

"Yo!" yelled Shawn, interupting my thoughts. He had spotted Terry and Butch.

"Yo," answered Butch. We waited as they walked up to us, Terry tossing a ball and catching it repeatedly as they came.

Beaky edged closer.

"Beat it, Norton," said Butch. "We don't want you around."

Beaky grinned nervously, revealing large yellow teeth. Then he moved about ten feet away. He cradled his new catcher's mitt in his arms.

"The way I figure," Butch said to the rest of us, "is that this last half hour of practice isn't going to make any difference to some of us."

Everyone's eyes moved to Shawn. We all knew Shawn would be the first to get cut from Rutledge.

Shawn stared at the muddy grass beneath his shoes. Then he looked back at us, his blue eyes blinking behind gold wire-rimmed glasses. He wrinkled his nose and shrugged.

At least Shawn knew where he stood, I thought, envying him for a second. He didn't have to wake up this morning with a knot in his stomach, and then force down breakfast in front of his mom and go off to school and put up with education, all the while knowing that at six o'clock his fate would be decided. Like Beaky, Shawn's fate was already decided. He only went out to take part in the preseason practices.

"The rest of us," said Butch reasonably, "like Terry and me, have to make sure we get our warm-up."

"How 'bout me?" I demanded.

"Oh, sure. You too, Scott," said Butch. "Let's spread out is all I'm saying. Then Shawn can pitch to one man at a time. That way we'll all get practice."

"Okay," I agreed. It still sounded like some kind of plan to leave me out.

We separated, with me in the middle between Terry and Butch, Shawn about ten yards away with the ball.

Shawn looked at the sky, looked at the ground, and shuffled his feet. He spit to one side. Then he wound up, aimed at the sun, and let go.

For a skinny little kid, he sure could throw high. The problem was he had no aim at all. The ball rose higher and higher, arced over our heads and started to fall.

Butch and Terry and I all ran to the same spot.

"It's mine!" screamed Terry.

He might be louder than anyone else his age on earth, but he was wrong. It was mine. I reached for it. It tipped off the end of my glove and into Butch's.

"Stupid cheap glove," I muttered. Feeling like a fool, I threw my glove on the ground and kicked it. "Piece of junk!" I kicked it again.

The glove slid and picked up about an inch of mud in the laces. I didn't care. Kicking it made me feel better.

4

"Cheap glove?" said Butch and laughed. He tossed the ball up and caught it easily. "You missed because of your glove?"

"Yeah," I said. "It's stiff. Nobody could catch with a glove like that."

"Anything you say," said Butch, grinning.

"Are you telling me you think that was my fault?"

"I'm telling you I know it was your fault," said Butch, tossing the ball again.

"Prissy Pritchard," shouted Terry. "Prissy Missy missed the ball."

I could feel the blood rush to my brain, filling it, making everything tense and confusing. Off to one side, Beaky made a sort of snorting noise through his huge nose.

"Cut it out!" I yelled.

"Catch," said Butch, pitching the ball past me to Terry.

"Catch!" said Terry, pitching it back.

"Think fast!" Butch acted as if he were going to throw the ball to me, then wheeled and tossed it to Terry.

Through tremendous effort, I managed not to yell at them. I tried to count to ten and only got to three. I was red hot and angry. I felt like one thousand bees, buzzing furiously.

"Prissy wants the ball," said Terry. He threw the ball so close to my head that it almost hit me.

"Ha, ha. Missed it!" yelled Beaky.

I swung in his direction. "Loudmouth!" I screamed.

"Ape ears," said Beaky right back.

"Ape ears?" repeated Butch, almost in a whisper.

5

Then he laughed. "Ape ears, ape ears," he chanted. He laughed some more. Then Terry laughed too. Even Shawn had a sort of foolish grin on his face.

"Ape ears," sneered Terry.

I ran at him, giving a rebel yell.

Terry took off. He is the fastest runner in the eighth grade. Even so, I almost had him. I chased him past the rickety old bleachers and around them, then over them once and out toward the parking lot.

I could never catch him at full speed in a million years. My lungs felt raw from trying and my legs were so weak that it was all I could do to stagger back to where the rest of the guys stood watching. At least I had control over my anger by then, or I thought I did.

As I passed Beaky Norton, he looked at me out of his big brown cowlike eyes and said, "Ape ears."

I lost it. I threw myself at him, and we both went down in a heap, Beaky on the bottom, me on top, Beaky yelling and me pounding him with all the strength I had.

Mostly I pounded him in the sides, while he roared and twisted and scrabbled in the mud, trying to get away from me.

"Fruit," I yelled, "Nerd," and a lot of other things. Then I sat up, my rear end on his skinny rib cage, one leg in the mud on either side of his body.

"Big-nose Norton," I roared, bringing my fist back for a super blow to his most outstanding feature.

A hand caught me by the wrist. Another grabbed the back of my collar. I was hauled upward and backward.

Beaky sat up, sniveling and wiping at his nose, tears forming in his cow's eyes.

I turned in fury, ready to punch whoever had stopped me.

The largest of the three coaches for Rutledge Rims was holding me by the collar. He made a sound of pure disgust, then dropped me into the mud and looked toward the other two coaches, who were standing together only a few feet away.

I groaned out loud. Everyone always said I was terrific at baseball, but I knew from experience that coaches don't like kids who fight.

I tried out for the team anyway, but I was one of the first kids cut, along with Beaky and Shawn. That was bad, but things got even worse when I got home that night. I knew my situation was serious as soon as I saw the stricken look on Mom's face.

"You've been fighting again," she said with a little gasp.

"There was a riot. I had to save myself."

"This is not funny, Scott," said my father, glaring at me from under bushy black eyebrows. "We told you what would happen the next time you got into a fight, and this is it. You just ran out of chances."

"No," I said. "No way! I'm not going near the mental health center. You have to be crazy!"

"You're the one who's crazy, Teenybopper," said Tina.

She's been calling me that ever since I turned thirteen. She knows I hate it. I started for her, my fists clenched.

"Scott Matthew!" said my father, his voice low and cold.

I took a deep breath, then another. "I'm not going," I said.

"You don't have to go to the center," said Mom. "I called several weeks ago to discuss your problem. You'll be referred to Dr. Wocoviak. You can go directly to his office." Her voice took on a pleading note.

"And you *are* going," said my father. "We've tried everything else."

"All right." I gave in. They *had* tried everything else: grounding, no television, no allowance. Nothing worked. A counselor wouldn't either.

"It's just a little problem," said Grandpa. "You'll get it solved."

My father frowned at him, and my mother got tight around her mouth the way she does sometimes when Grandpa interferes with advice. I didn't mind though. It was nice to have Grandpa on my side.

I was still thinking about that ugly scene with my parents when Beaky's window flew open with a horrible squealing noise. Beaky stuck his head out.

"I brought back your catcher's mitt," I said. I had taken it for revenge.

"In the middle of the night?"

"You want it?"

"Sure."

"Then come down and get it." I made my voice friendly, but Beaky was suspicious anyway.

"Toss it up," he said.

I pretended to try a couple of times, making sure the mitt went nowhere near the window.

"You can leave it on the porch," he said.

"The rats will get it." I didn't know if there were any rats around or not, but it sounded good.

"Bring it to school tomorrow."

"No. I came way over here so you wouldn't worry all night. If you don't come get it, I'm going to drop it in a ditch somewhere."

"Okay," he finally answered after a long pause. His window went screaming down and banged.

I winced, waiting for lights to go on all over the house. They didn't, and after a few seconds I relaxed.

"Hurry up, Beaky," I muttered under my breath. "I'm going to murder you."

2

"Why'd you come over in the middle of the night?" asked Beaky when at last he joined me on the lawn at the back of his house. His voice was high-pitched and frightened.

"I want to talk to you." What I really wanted was to beat on him privately, without anyone butting in.

"Couldn't it wait until tomorrow?" Beaky shivered. He had pulled jeans on over his pajama bottoms. The jeans were riding at high tide as usual. His light pajamas stuck out several inches beneath them. He was also wearing a dark jacket. His nose glimmered white in the moonlight.

"I couldn't sleep," I said. "All I could think about was how you wrecked my life."

"Me?" squeaked Beaky. "How?"

"You got me cut from Rutledge Rims," I said, "and that is only half of it."

There was a short silence while Beaky considered this. He sniffed and rubbed the sleeve of his right arm under his nose. Then he said, "What's the other half?"

"None of your business," I told him. All of a sudden I was very depressed. My plan was to beat up on Beaky, and now I wasn't even mad. How could I hit him if I wasn't mad? I decided that I had to stall a couple of minutes, keep him talking. Sooner or later he would say something to irritate me, and then I would pulverize him.

"Are you going to beat on me?" asked Beaky, his voice small and scared.

"Naw," I lied. "I just want to talk to you a little." Suddenly I shook with cold, almost dropping the mitt. "How can it be so freezing!" I burst out. "It's supposed to be spring."

"We could go in my house to talk," said Beaky hopefully. "We could have a cup of hot chocolate."

"No way. Let's walk." I grabbed him by one sleeve and practically dragged him away from the house, toward a little grove of trees that divided the Nortons' lot from a big group of condominiums some builder was putting up.

It wasn't one bit warmer in the trees. Beaky sneezed violently and rubbed at his nose.

"I never was out this late before," he said.

Figuring he would scream when I hit him, I dragged him farther from the house. We broke through the trees and into an open space at the back of the condominiums. In the pink glow from a security light, they

11

looked almost finished, but they still had that empty isolated air places get when they're totally uninhabited.

"I know," said Beaky, cheering up. "We can go in there. At least we'll be out of the wind." When I hesitated, he added, "Come on. The middle door in the back is sometimes left open when they go off work at four."

I shoved my right fist deep into my jacket pocket. I wanted it to be plenty flexible for beating on Beaky. Then I followed him past six doors to a flat door set even with the cement-block wall. He messed a little with the knob, and the door swung open.

"Come on," he repeated and was inside before I had a chance to answer.

Beaky must have eyes like a cat. Either that or he had been inside the place so often that he knew exactly where he was going. I grabbed the back of his jacket to follow him, but even so I tripped over things and bumped into walls. I had a terrible time managing the steps, but once we reached the top, everything was suddenly better. The floor was a smooth terrazzo beneath my feet, and some light leaked out of the door Beaky led me to.

"They're working their way down from the top," said Beaky proudly, as if he owned the place. "The third and fourth floors are painted, carpeted, drapes, everything. Well, almost everything. They don't have equipment like the televisions and fireplace stuff and refrigerators installed. Down here they're putting in carpet, but they haven't got to the drapes."

"I'm not interested in buying," I said. We must have been in a living room. An enormous window let in enough light for me to see the pale oval of Beaky's face. His dark eyes looked like chunks of chocolate in a bar of nougat.

"They aren't for sale. They're for rent, and they're real expensive. My grandmother says the contractors will never fill them."

"I didn't come all the way over here in the middle of the night to talk about real estate," I said nastily, reminding myself that I was here to make an example of Beaky, trying to work myself into a rage.

Beaky didn't say anything. After a couple of seconds, I went on. "What was it you called me this afternoon?"

"I don't remember," he said sullenly.

"Sure you do," I said. "I only want to hear it again."

"Ape ears," he said unwillingly.

I felt familiar anger course through my body. "What?" I asked. "I didn't hear you."

"Ape ears," said Beaky a little louder.

A quivering anger ran through me, turning me warm. Any moment now, my temper would take over.

"Ape ears are round and black and look like pieces of old tire tread," I said pleasantly, letting my anger build silently so as not to warn him. "I know. I looked at one this evening in a *National Geographic.*"

Beaky cleared his throat, then snickered.

"Why did you call me that?"

"Well," said Beaky, "when you were trying to catch that ball you went into a crouch with your legs all bent and funny, and your arms seemed extra long." He hesitated. "Then I noticed how your ears are sort of round and stick straight out from under your baseball cap—"

13

That did it. I lunged at him, catching his waist in a midair flying tackle. We went down in a heap on the carpet, rolling over and over.

Beaky did better on carpet than he did in mud. One minute I had him, holding with one hand, pounding with the other. The next minute, he was gone.

I scrambled to my hands and knees and peered around the room, breathing hard. He hadn't escaped out the door. It was behind me. My eyes swiveled in the dark room, trying to locate him.

"Come out, Norton, you coward," I snarled.

He didn't answer. There wasn't anyplace he could be hiding in the room except behind the fireplace, which seemed to have its back built into a hallway. I started toward it, still on my hands and knees.

"You come out or I'll break every bone in your body," I threatened. Then I held my breath, trying to locate him by sound. If he was behind the fireplace, I didn't want him to get the jump on me.

There was no sound at all. I had a sudden vision of both Beaky and me holding our breath till we passed out.

In the stillness of the night, I heard a sharp *clonk*, then a muffled sound, like the door of a truck being eased open.

"Beaky!" I whispered. "There's somebody out there!"

In a second, Beaky was beside me, his eyes wide and anxious in the moonlight. We scurried across the carpet on our hands and knees, eased up and peered out the window.

There was a dark van parked at the service entrance we had entered. It had a bubble skylight on its roof, and the back doors stood open. Besides that, I couldn't see much.

We waited a couple of seconds. Then a man appeared and adjusted something on the service door so it stayed open.

The man went inside the building. In a couple of minutes, he was back again with another man. They carried a large white rectangle between them. While we watched, they wrestled it into the van and went back inside the building.

"They must be workmen," said Beaky. "They must have come back to pick up a shipment."

"In the middle of the night? I must have hit you too hard on the head," I muttered. "Besides, what are they doing taking refrigerators anyway?"

"I don't know. You can't expect me to answer everything."

"You dragged me in here," I said, "and now you got me all set up for breaking and entering. Those men catch us, and we're in big trouble."

We watched while the men loaded a second refrigerator and a third one. Suddenly aware that the men were stealing, I sank down on the carpet, my back to the window.

"I wonder why they took the refrigerators out of the crates," said Beaky. "Why leave a whole bunch of empty crates in the basement?"

I sighed heavily and rolled my eyes at the ceiling.

"Those men are *stealing* the refrigerators," he said at last, "and leaving the crates so no one will know they are missing."

"Norton, you're a genius."

"We have to stop them."

"For a genius, you are pretty dumb."

"We have to get out of here and call the police." He grabbed my arm, his head close to mine. I could smell his breath. It stank of garlic.

"And how are we going to explain what we were doing here in the middle of the night?"

"We can say we couldn't sleep and we decided to go for a walk."

I groaned, then clamped a hand over my mouth. Those men weren't making any noise, and I sure didn't want them to notice us.

"We have to do something," said Beaky, tugging at my arm.

"Right now we have to hole up and keep quiet. If those guys catch us, they aren't about to pat us on the shoulders and send us home safe to Mommy."

Beaky slid down beside me on the carpet. We must have sat there next to each other for another half hour, while I tried to think and Beaky whined about being afraid. Despite all my worry and Beaky's sniveling, I did manage to come to a conclusion. There was no way we could tell on those men without being caught ourselves. I didn't know about Beaky, but as for me, my life was already too complicated without having to explain what I was doing in the condominiums in the middle of the night.

At last I heard the purr of the van's engine. I edged up on my knees. It was moving away in total darkness, its lights out. As I watched, it turned onto Morrison Street. After about a hundred yards, the headlights went on.

"What'll we do?" asked Beaky.

I gave him the steadiest glare I could under the circumstances.

"Norton," I said, "you tell one person about this and you'll be wearing that nose of yours growing out the back of your head."

3

So much happened to me in the next week that I almost forgot about that night at Beaky's—almost but not quite. I convinced myself that the refrigerator thieves had nothing to do with me.

What did have to do with me is that Shawn convinced me to go out for a different baseball team. It was called Lyttons Union Co-op, but everyone called it Lyttons' Losers because guys our age who had been cut from the other Hot Stove League teams could join it.

I wasn't quite certain how I felt about Lyttons' Losers. It was a real humiliation to be on that team, but maybe it was better than no team at all. At least I would have a chance to play baseball, even if it wasn't with Butch and Terry and all the other kids who knew how.

18

The other thing was that I had my first meeting with the counselor. His office was in the basement of a boys' dormitory at the college, about six blocks from our house. I walked there one afternoon after school and sat waiting outside his office in a large room lit by fluorescent lights and filled with beat-up furniture.

I felt a lot like I do when I have to wait at the dentist, sort of sick and scared. To take my mind off things, I tried to think about my grandpa. He was the one who needed a counselor, I decided. He had worse problems than I did.

They began about three years ago, when Grandmother decided to go to Tucson for her asthma. Grandpa went out with her on vacation. She improved so much that when he came home, she stayed on for a couple of months, just until the ragweed season was over, she said.

The ragweed season came and went, but Grandma never did come home. She met some old guy out there and divorced Grandpa and married him.

Grandpa started hanging around our house a lot, after work and weekends. He said he was too young to join Golden Agers' organizations and too old for the swinging singles. He said he never expected to be at an awkward age in his late fifties.

There was a creaking noise from behind the office door, like someone getting out of a desk chair. I stopped thinking about my grandfather and got into a cold sweat over myself.

What kind of a man was this counselor? My mother said he wasn't a regular with the mental health center, but taught child psychology at the college, plus experimental psychology and some other stuff. I only hoped he didn't get the experimental and the child psychology mixed up and mess up my brain.

"Scott," said the short balding man. "Would you like to come in? I'm Dr. Wocoviak."

All of a sudden I was terrified. Sweat ran down my back, soaking my shirt between my shoulder blades. My heart ran wild, and I felt very weak in the knees. "Hi," I said feebly, following him into his inner sanctum. Tell him nothing, I warned myself, nothing that can be used against you.

"Sit down." He smiled again, motioning to a chair on the other side of a big desk littered with papers.

We sat, staring at each other. Then he leaned back in his chair and swiveled, pretending to look at a framed picture of the earth taken from outer space.

I eyed him warily. He was clean-shaven except for a bushy mustache. He had on horn-rimmed glasses and wore a blue shirt with the sleeves rolled up. He also had on a dark blue tie with a picture of a trout leaping for a fly on it.

What kind of a man wants to snoop into other people's minds? I wondered. How good is this guy anyway? I had my suspicions. My parents buy lots of things at a discount—my baseball glove, my sneakers, now maybe even my counselor. How was I ever going to get my head in order with a discount counselor? I glared at him.

Then I sniffed at the air in the room. There was a sort of sweetish smell that wasn't helping my queasy stomach. It could have been men's perfume.

"I think that today we should get to know each other a little better," he said quietly. "We already know each

20

other's names. I work here at the college. I'm a teacher. Now why don't you tell me about yourself?"

"I'm a kid and I go to school," I said.

"Okay." His voice suggested that he approved of this. Then he added, "I understand you have a bit of a problem."

"I'm a nut case."

"Hardly." He looked sympathetic. "You do seem to get into a lot of fights, but that might be only a symptom. You have to find out what's causing the problem, and I'm here to help you."

"Yeah," I said.

There was a little silence. I wondered if he was paid by the minute and his meter was running even when he wasn't doing anything. I glanced quickly around the room. He didn't even have a couch like counselors do on television.

When he finally decided to stop wasting my time and my parents' money, Dr. Wocoviak asked me a bunch of questions about myself and my family, school and my friends, what I like to do in my free time, stuff like that. The interview went pretty well, with me doing a lot more talking than I had planned on. Finally I wound down and sat watching him, wondering what would happen next. There was another one of those little silences while I waited.

"Let's understand one thing," he said at last, leaning forward and putting his hands flat on his desk, palms down. "I'm not trying to change you, to make you have a different personality. I'm here to help you to find out why you have this problem and to help you beat it."

I didn't answer.

"Just think of me as sort of a coach," he said. He

seemed to like that idea. "Like in basketball or baseball. We get together and we talk about how the game is going and how you might play a little better. Okay?"

"Okay," I said.

He glanced at his watch. "I have to check on my lab assistant now. She's new this week. Tell you what. Between now and your next appointment, I'd like you to try to analyze why you get into fights, what sets you off."

That was dumb. I knew what caused me to lose my temper. It was the other kids. If they wouldn't tease me, I would have complete control of myself.

"The other kids," I said out loud. The more I acted as if I were going along with the whole counseling scheme, the sooner Dr. Wocoviak and my parents would decide I didn't need it anymore.

"But why do they make you mad? Think about it. You might make some notes on a piece of paper. We'll talk about that the next time, and if you think about anything else you'd like to discuss, we'll talk about that too."

"That's all?" I was surprised, and my voice showed it.

"That's all for today. This is only a sort of preliminary interview, for us to get used to each other."

"Okay."

"Is this the best time for you, or would you rather come after dinner in the evenings?"

"This is all right," I heard myself say.

"See you next week then."

Dr. Wocoviak didn't even tell me not to get into any fights, but I hadn't been doing too badly on my own. It had been almost a week since my battle with Beaky, and I hadn't gotten into any scrapes, not one. Not unless I counted that little session with Butch. He'd called me Prissy Pritchard, and I'd had to slap him around a little, nothing major.

Actually I hadn't even wanted to fight except whenever I saw Beaky. I thought I'd put Beaky Norton at the top of a list of things that caused me to fight. I'd make the stupid list and stay away from Beaky, and then after a week or two the counselor would decide I was cured, and I could go on with my life as always.

I felt almost happy as I left Dr. Wocoviak's office. I whistled through my front teeth and walked the way I do when I feel big and strong and in charge.

4

We had our first practice for Lytton's Losers that evening. By the time Grandpa dropped Shawn and me off at the practice field, which was way on the other side of town, I already had two items on my list of what made me fight. The first was Beaky; the second was Tina. She caught me with Dad's razor before dinner and ran all over the house screaming "Teenybopper's shaving! Teenybopper's shaving!"

Shawn piled out of the car at the practice field as proud as if we were on a regular team instead of one made up of all the rejects in our age category. I followed more slowly.

"The practices last about two hours," I told Grandpa in case he didn't want to hang around.

"I think I'll stay and watch for a while," he said. "It's nice this evening, and I can use the fresh air."

"All right." I trudged over to join the gang of boys gathered around a couple of coaches. I shouldered myself into the mob next to Shawn and a little behind him so I didn't block his view. Shawn twisted to glance at me, wrinkling his nose like a rabbit as always. Then he looked back at the coaches.

One of the coaches was short and sort of dumpy, his waist the fattest part of his body. He wore a faded orange baseball cap, and his brown eyes were very sad looking. He didn't look as if he could know a whole lot about baseball or anything else for that matter. While I watched him, he tugged at the waist of his pants, lifted them, and let them drop onto his hips again. The right side of his plaid shirt flipped out of his waistband and hung flapping. He didn't seem to notice it.

The other coach was all energy. He was about the same height as the fat coach, but he was trim, almost wiry, muscular for a guy with gray hair. He kept hopping from foot to foot as if he had to go to the bathroom. He also kept smacking his right fist into the palm of the glove on his left hand.

"Let's go. Let's go," he shouted, only it sounded like "Let's gue. Let's gue."

"Somehow I don't think this is going to be the team that wins the trophy," I muttered at the back of Shawn's head. "I think we're going to come out here every evening and work hard and end up right where we started, at the bottom of the league."

"So what have we got to lose?" whispered Shawn over his shoulder.

"A lot of baseball games."

"Now that man right there is Mr. Mathais," yelled the wiry coach all of a sudden. "And he is one of the finest coaches in all of Hot Stove League. We are lucky to have him."

Mr. Mathais took off his orange baseball cap, scratched at the top of his head, and put it back on.

"And I am Bob Baker. You boys can call me Bob or Mr. Baker, but when I call you, you'd better come first time." He scowled ferociously. "You all understand?"

When nobody answered, he added, "Now no one is cut from this team, and no one is going to be kept from playing."

"Spare us the sermon," said a kid beside me. Another kid snickered, and a third one belched.

"We are all here to play baseball," said Bob Baker, still yelling. "So let's play! Spread out and take the positions you worked on during preseason practice. We'll change things around later. Right now, let's mo-o-ve out! I say MOVE!"

I headed toward third base, while Shawn ran to the outfield where he could do as little damage as possible. When I reached my base, I turned toward home plate to see what the coaches were up to.

Standing there was a familiar gawky figure, a huge catcher's mitt dangling at the end of one skinny arm. Beaky Norton had signed up for Lyttons'. While I stared in horror, he lifted his free hand and waved at me.

I acted as if I didn't see him, staring at the ground, the sky, scratching my nose. Then I talked with the other two guys who had also decided to play third base.

In a couple of minutes, Mr. Mathais came around.

"You're navy team," he said to me. Then he told the second kid, "You're orange team, third base.

You're orange team, first base," he told the other one.

I was lucky. Beaky was orange. At least during our practice sessions, we wouldn't be on the same team. I didn't have to sit on the same bench with him.

Actually the practice went pretty well until I came up to bat the first time. Beaky was behind me, catching, but I ignored him, concentrating on the ball just the way I'd been taught.

Orange had a terrific pitcher. He threw only one ball. The next pitch was straight down the middle. I was expecting another ball and didn't swing.

"Strike one!" yelled Bob Baker.

The next pitch came sizzling down the middle too. I swung hard, but the ball curved at the last second. I heard it thunk into Beaky's mitt.

"Missed it, Ape Ears," said Beaky.

I gripped the bat, practically blind with rage. It took all my strength of will not to turn and slam that bat down over Beaky's head. If I had, in ten seconds Beaky would have known if there really was a heaven.

Naturally I struck out.

Beaky didn't call me Ape Ears again, which was a lucky thing. I don't know if I could have managed not to kill him the second time around. The rest of practice went pretty well. I got two hits—one a long fly, the other a two-base hit.

Grandpa stayed the whole practice. So did a couple of mothers, but he was the only man there. He stood off to one side and talked some with the mothers.

We went the full two hours. Afterward Bob Baker gave us another pep talk, and then Mr. Mathais handed out schedules.

That was when Beaky decided to approach me. He

edged up close, looking at me as if I were some sort of dangerous animal, and said, "I have to talk to you, Scott."

"So talk." At least he had called me by my name.

"Not here." His eyes slid around uneasily. "In private."

"About what?"

"About the other evening."

It took me a couple of seconds to realize what he meant.

"It's important," he pressed.

"Tell me now." I moved a little to one side with him, although I didn't want the other kids to think we were friends.

"I can't tell you now," he insisted, a stubborn expression in his cow eyes. "Come on over tonight."

"I have to go right home," I told him. "I had to go someplace after school today, and I have a report due tomorrow in social studies."

"Well—" he hesitated. "You can come later."

I sighed. At least it wasn't cold out. I wouldn't freeze if I went back to the Nortons' in the middle of the night.

"Meet me on your back lawn at 1 A.M.," I said.

"Right, man!" said Beaky. He turned and hustled away before I could change my mind. He went over to where my grandfather stood and said something to a tall lady with dark hair. Then he and the lady headed toward a green Honda hatchback.

"Let's go," said Shawn, coming up beside me, only now he said it "Let's gue," like Coach Bob Baker.

I thought of going home and doing my paper for

28

social studies, and I groaned. Then I thought of going over to Beaky's in the middle of the night, and I groaned even louder. Then I remembered that I had a third item for my list of what makes me fight. It was being called Ape Ears.

5

About 12:40 that night, I sneaked out of the house and headed toward the Nortons'. I kept to the bushes for the first block and then walked right out on the sidewalk as if it were early evening. I figured if anyone saw me from a house, they would think I was an adult who couldn't sleep. If I saw any cars, particularly police cars, I would dive in the bushes.

I saw only one—police car, that is. I saw three other cars too, but none of the people in them saw me. There weren't many people around in our end of town that late on a weeknight.

I walked by the houses on the quiet empty streets, and I didn't see anyone else outside. I saw an occasional person in a house and the blue flicker of a television set now and then, but not one other person walking. That was sort of too bad for them. It was so pleasant out, quiet and peaceful. I leaned my head back and looked at the stars in the sky. I couldn't see nearly as many as I could on a camping trip to the woods, but there were plenty for our town. I could even locate the Big Dipper.

I walked on, feeling good, like some kind of intelligent animal, with all my senses open and alert. Things smelled better at night, or maybe I was only more aware of them. They felt better too. It was warm, getting on toward summer at last, and there was the tiniest breeze, barely noticeable.

Because I moved as silently as possible, I could hear the night sounds of insects and the far away twanging of something that might have been a frog. I don't know if it was a frog; I thought maybe frogs hung around their burrows or dens or whatever until June, but it sounded like one.

Then I covered one entire block pretending I was an undercover agent in the outskirts of Moscow, being trailed by the KGB. I scurried from tree to tree, bush to bush, checking out the area and keeping my body tense, ready for action, my right hand always free to reach for my gun. I was a superb machine, tightly tuned by the U.S. government to fight its enemies at home and in hostile foreign lands. Enemy agents were everywhere, ready to terminate me on sight. They would never capture me alive, and it was only the rarest of execution teams that could hope to have me within their gun sights for a fraction of a second.

I could never pretend all that in the middle of the day. Even Grandpa would say I should see a counselor.

By the time I arrived at Beaky's, I was positively

grateful to him for making me go out that night. I couldn't see why people wasted their time sleeping at all. I thought that maybe Beaky and I should arrange to meet more often in the middle of the night. I would prefer to hang out with Shawn, but Shawn sleeps in the same room as his older brother, and it would be very difficult for him to escape his house undetected.

There was no sign of Beaky. I walked to the middle of his back lawn and stared up at his window. I waited for a couple of minutes and then decided I was going to have to use the old stones-at-the-window trick. Obviously Beaky had fallen asleep.

"PSSST!"

"Yaah!" I yelled, almost jumping out of my skin. I took a couple of rapid steps, ready to run, and then my brain started functioning again.

"Beaky! What are you trying to do, give me a heart attack?" Beaky came out of the trees behind me.

"I thought I'd better hide in case someone woke up and looked out a window."

"It's a wonder the whole town isn't awake," I said. I'd yelled loud enough. I glanced toward the house. "Your parents must sleep like the dead."

"Their room's at the front of the house," he said. "Come on," and he started off through the trees.

"Where?"

"To the condominiums."

I trailed after him until I realized I was following Beaky, and that didn't seem right; so I pushed in front of him.

The condominiums were absolutely deserted, the way they had been the first night we were there.

"Did you get me over here to show me something?"

I asked when Beaky and I stopped behind a bush at the edge of the trees. We stood motionless, breathing quietly in the still night, looking at the back of the nearest building.

"I have this plan—" he began.

I groaned.

"Just listen. We can't let those guys get away with it."

"We can't?" Even as I protested, the undercover agent lurking deep within me became more and more interested.

"No way. First I thought of making an anonymous phone call, and then I thought of writing a letter to the police, but that wouldn't do any good. They'd only start running more patrols around here and scare the men off," he said. "Then I thought that what we have to do is to get more information, maybe the make of the van or the license plate number. Then we would have some real evidence."

"Maybe I could bring my camera and take some color snaps," I said sarcastically.

"They'd probably notice the flash." Beaky is absolutely impervious to sarcasm. It could be from growing up with a nose like his.

"When are we going to do this?" I asked.

"Tonight, I hope."

"Did you set up an appointment so they would be sure to be here?"

This time Beaky actually noticed the sarcasm. "Of course not," he said very stiffly. "I checked the service door before baseball practice, and it was open. I've checked it every night this week, and this was the first night they left it unlocked."

I whistled through my teeth. Norton wasn't so dumb after all.

"I also looked inside and there was a bunch of new crates. Stoves, I think. They're too big for televisions and the wrong shape for refrigerators."

"So we wait here, and when they're inside getting one of the stoves, we sneak up and get their plate number."

"Right."

"Right-o," I echoed cheerfully. "Maybe we'll get a reward."

"And our pictures in the paper."

I wasn't certain I wanted my picture in the paper with Beaky, but I didn't say so.

We stood in the bush and watched the back of the condominium. After about fifteen minutes, it began to get boring. I told myself that undercover men were often on stakeout for days, weeks, but I was not that kind of undercover man. I was more the kind that held running battles through the streets of Rome.

Finally, when an hour had passed, I started complaining. It was after two. If I wanted any sleep at all, I had to go home soon.

"I guess they aren't coming," said Beaky at last, when it was going on four. "Maybe the van broke down or something."

"Maybe their wives wouldn't let them out." I yawned. By this time I was slumped in the bush, my rear end wet from the damp ground. Beaky was still standing, his eyes fixed on the service door like an Irish setter on point.

"We'll have to come back tomorrow night," said Beaky.

This snapped me wide-awake. "Hey," I said, scrambling to my feet. "We have to sleep some time. We have our health to think of."

"I always sleep in language arts," said Beaky proudly.

"Besides that. At night."

"Suppose I keep checking the door. If it's open, we watch. If it isn't, we don't."

"All right," I agreed reluctantly. "But if it's open too many nights, we're going to have to split up and take turns."

"You mean wait out here *alone?*" Beaky sounded absolutely horrified.

"Yeah." I choked back a laugh.

"Good night, Norton," I said, giving him a friendly smack on the shoulder.

The smack almost knocked Beaky over, but he took it the way it was intended. "Good night, Pritchard," he said professionally.

For that little moment, Ape Ears Pritchard and Beaky Norton were a team.

6

It was another eight days before Beaky and I spotted the men again. By that time, we had spent two more nights hiding in the bushes, one of them in the rain. I had gone to all my baseball practices. I also had fallen asleep twice in language arts and once in math. I met with my counselor again. Although he wasn't doing me much good, I had to admit he wasn't the nerd I'd thought at first.

For one thing, he didn't pretend he was my pal or talk to me about baseball and stuff as if he knew all about it. He didn't give me any lectures either. What he did do, first thing, was ask me if I'd thought about what made me mad.

"I wrote a list," I said, pulling it out of my pocket and handing it over.

He looked down over the list, which had grown to

seventeen causes, including Beaky and Tina and Ape Ears.

"Tina is your sister?" he asked, as if he already knew.

"Yeah."

"And Beaky is a friend of yours?"

I hesitated so long that he looked up from the paper.

"I guess so," I said. "We're working on a project together."

"And Butch and Terry and Frank, Jason and Sam."

"Butch and Terry are friends. The other ones are kids at school."

"But they make you mad?"

"Sometimes."

He pulled at his lower lip with the fingers of one hand. Then he put the little finger of the same hand into his right ear and twisted it. I wondered if maybe he had a gnat in there. That had happened to me once, and my mother had taken me to the doctor to have my ear irrigated.

If there was a gnat in his ear, it wasn't bothering him much. He studied the paper a few more minutes and then said, "Is this Ape Ears another friend of yours?"

I could feel my cheeks get hot. "That's me," I said.

"You mean you get mad at yourself?"

"No. I get mad when people call me that. Beaky started it, but now some of the guys on my baseball team call me that too." I could feel the slow boil that I'd been trying to keep on simmer all week get hotter.

Dr. Wocoviak didn't notice. He put the paper flat on his desk, then shoved it back at me. It slid, and I caught it before it cleared the desk and went on the floor.

"Tell me about your week," he said.

Aha, I thought. Gotcha. Finally my counselor begins to act as if he knows what he's doing. I only wished he had a couch for me to lie down on. I was pretty tired.

"You mean when I got into fights?"

"You can tell me about that too, but I'd like to hear about your whole week—what happened from day to day, where you went, what you did."

"Well, most days I went to school and ate dinner and went to ball practice and then did my homework or watched the tube and went to bed."

He didn't look impressed. He waited patiently, fiddling with a pencil, his meter running.

I took a deep breath. "In school I like mostly social studies and gym and language arts," I said, "but I've been having trouble in language arts lately. I keep falling asleep. I did a paper on the Constitution for social studies last week, but I didn't get my grade for it yet."

All of a sudden it was easy. I didn't know I could talk that much. I talked about school and my family and especially Tina, how she's always telling on me and calling me names. Then I told him about ball practice, how Beaky called me Ape Ears and I almost killed him, but I didn't tell him about meeting Beaky to watch the condominiums. I explained that our coaches have this weird philosophy that it isn't that important to win games, but what is important is to improve at playing and to be on time for practice and to observe the rules of good sportsmanship. Also, I told him about Beaky Norton's grandmother.

I had noticed her that first day when we were assigned positions and given our schedules. She was talking to my grandfather, and at the time I thought she was somebody's mother. It wasn't until three days later that I saw her up close, and I realized that she was a little old to be someone's mother—someone my age, I mean. It wouldn't be *impossible*, but I don't personally know any kids with mothers that old.

Grandmother Norton was very tall and slender. I didn't know if her clothes had cost a lot or not, but they looked as if they did. Her eyes were a dark brown, and her skin wasn't much wrinkled but it was a bit loose looking. The hair on her head was black and curly like the hair on Beaky's legs. On her, it looked good.

"Hello, Scott," she said. Her voice was low and husky with a little bounce in it.

"Hi," I said.

"Scott, this is Mrs. Norton, Beaky's grandmother," said my grandfather. He looked from me to her, and his eyes had this sort of aware look, as if maybe life wasn't all that disappointing anymore. "She and I have been going for coffee while you boys practice."

Mrs. Norton smiled, revealing even white teeth. I wondered if they were fake or if they were her own. They looked very strong, good for biting things.

Then Shawn came up, and we were all standing around in a cozy little group.

"Well," said Mrs. Norton. "Do you boys think you can come up with a couple of winning games?"

"No," said Shawn, looking very serious. "Our team is the losers."

Mrs. Norton gave a little laugh. It was low and husky, like her voice.

Grandpa looked at her as if she had just done something absolutely fascinating.

"I'm waiting for my grandson," she said. "He's on the

39

team too." She glanced over Shawn's head. "There he is. Stanley! Oh, Stanley!"

Evidently Beaky didn't realize she was calling him because he kept walking toward the parking lot. It was no wonder. No one calls him Stanley, not even the teachers. Probably Beaky has forgotten he ever had another name.

I didn't tell my counselor about Mrs. Norton's laugh either. I went straight from meeting her to the rest of my week, which wasn't as interesting as the first part, but he listened to it anyway. I told him about the little scuffle Terry and I had during cafeteria. I'd tripped over Terry's big feet, and he'd made a big deal out of it. I also told him Frank had been calling me Ape Ears, but I hadn't hit him even once. Finally I ran out of things to say.

Dr. Wocoviak patted his shirt pockets as if he were searching for a pack of cigarettes.

"Oh, I almost forgot," I said. "We got our team uniforms too. We're going to get our picture taken either at the end of this week or the beginning of next. The coaches are setting up some practice games with other teams too."

He nodded. He picked up his pencil and fiddled with it some more. Then his eyes went to the list I still held in my hands.

"Thinking about your week, and considering the list you made there," he said, "I'd like you to concentrate on two things between now and our next appointment. I'd like you to think about what makes you angry. You have a list there, but it's really only a list of people's names. Do you get mad at these people all the time? You said some of them are your friends."

40

"No," I said. I thought a couple of seconds. "Things happen and my temper takes over."

"What actually happens? That is important. What happens to make your temper take over?"

"Mostly because kids call me stuff. They make fun of me."

"Do they make fun of other people?"

"Sure." I shifted uncomfortably.

"All right. Then try to think of *why* you react the way you do when they make fun of you."

He sounded a lot like my grandpa, but I guess I could manage to think about that part of it. It wasn't as if he expected me to write a research paper or anything.

"Really think about it," he said, looking straight at me, his stare very intense and powerful.

"Did you ever hypnotize anyone?" I asked.

"What?" He laughed, sounding a lot like Mrs. Norton.

"I have an idea. If you can hypnotize people, then you can hypnotize me not to fight and I won't get into any more trouble."

"That would be nice," he agreed, "but I'm not so certain that it would be a good long-term solution. I'm not saying it's never been done; I'm only saying I don't think it's the best solution."

"Just asking." Personally, I didn't see anything wrong with the easy way, but if he wanted to keep meeting, it was all right with me. His fee wasn't coming out of my allowance.

"Now I also want you to think about what losing your temper gets you. You might put this down on paper too. Think—either before you get into a fight or afterward—how that fight affected your life, for good or for bad. Analyze the situation and control it."

"I think I'd rather be hypnotized."

"Wouldn't we all," he said, his hands once again patting his pockets. "See you next week, Scott."

7

That night it rained. I stood in the bushes watching the condominiums with Beaky and telling myself that the life of an international counterespionage agent was not for me. I was definitely headed for a job behind a desk, preferably some place in a desert.

Meanwhile, I was stuck listening to Beaky whine about losing his slicker and trying to ignore the little trickle of rain that ran steadily off the back of my cap and down my neck. It kept me awake. It also kept me cold and very miserable.

Beaky wasn't a whole lot better off, although he'd borrowed his mother's raincoat. It was long and tan and fitted at the waist with a belt. He's also borrowed her rain hat, which matched the coat. The hat had a soft crown and a wide brim which constantly dripped water all around, some of which struck Beaky's nose on the way to the ground. He had tied the hat strings under his chin in a small neat bow.

I eyed him in the pale pink glow from the faraway security light. In that hat and raincoat, his shoulders hunched and his nose protruding into the drizzle, Beaky looked like the ugliest woman on earth.

"Let's face it," I said. "Those guys aren't coming tonight. Probably they will never show up again. They've given up a life of crime and have retired to Florida."

"They have to come," insisted Beaky. "More stuff arrived today. I checked before ball practice. Some of the crates are pried open."

"They probably *would* pick this kind of weather," I said out loud. "It would be safe all right. Nobody but a fool would be out on a night like this."

All of a sudden, as if the idea had occurred to him right that second, Beaky said, "Why don't we wait inside?"

"Too dangerous. They might decide to look around."

"But it's wet out here!"

"You noticed."

"I already have a cold," he said, and sneezed as if to prove it. "My nose is all stuffed up."

With Beaky, that would be a major problem.

"Okay," I agreed. "I guess if they didn't catch us the last time, they won't tonight either."

Keeping a careful watch in the dripping night, we sneaked across the rear parking lot and through the service door. I followed Beaky up the stairs and trailed him to the apartment where we had been before.

"Take off your shoes," said Beaky, stopping at the door.

"Why? It's carpeted. Besides, I'm wearing sneakers. I won't make any noise."

"They're wet. You want to ruin the new carpet?"

I took off my shoes. We both did. We carried them in with us, then stripped off our raincoats and sat on the soft rug under the window.

Immediately I felt more like a human being. I sighed and stretched, then curled into a little ball.

Beaky blew his nose forty or fifty times. Then he began rummaging in the pockets of his mother's raincoat, looking for more tissues. After a few seconds, he pulled out a pack of cigarettes.

"Mom never goes anywhere without her cigarettes," he said. "Want one?"

"No," I yawned. "I don't want to die of lung cancer."

Evidently Beaky didn't either, as he put the cigarettes back in the pocket.

I was vaguely aware of his crawling around in the dark and then, later, coming over to join me on the rug under the window.

We fell sound asleep.

It wasn't the *thunk* of a van door opening that got our attention that time. It was the sound of men's voices coming from inside the building, directly below where we were sleeping.

"What's that?" whispered Beaky, coming awake the same moment I did.

"Shh!" Fortunately his voice had been low and full of sleep. The floor beneath us wasn't very well insulated. Although the men weren't talking very loudly, every word was clear.

"I tell you I heard something," one of them was insisting.

"And I didn't."

I held my breath, trying to keep absolutely silent. Beside me, Beaky was wiggling his nose in an alarming way. His mouth was half-open.

"Aaa-CHOO!" Beaky sneezed. It sounded like a cannon going off.

"There!" said the first man. "Somebody *is* in here."

"I didn't hear anything." The other man sounded very tired, as if he were fed up with a life of crime, sneaking around in the middle of the night, hauling refrigerators and stoves. "But if it will make you feel any better, we'll check it out."

Beaky and I looked at each other in the dim light from the window. Then we began pulling on our shoes, dragging on our rain gear. If we had to run, we'd better be ready.

"Hide in the bathroom," whispered Beaky.

"No. We have to get out of here!"

"But they're coming up the stairs!" His fingers fumbled at the strings on the rain hat.

I hesitated, listening. They weren't coming up the stairs. They had arrived.

"That mud on the floor wasn't there when I left this afternoon," said one of the men.

A beam of light appeared in a line under the apartment door.

Beaky gave a little whine and grabbed me by one arm. He was a whole head taller than I was, and in spite of his leanness, must have outweighed me. I thought my legs would buckle under the weight he put on that one arm.

"Let go!" I hissed, trying to pry him loose.

It was no use. Beaky only grabbed with his other hand too and turned his head toward the window, shutting his eyes tightly.

The door flew open with a crash, and the light blazed into the room, flickered over walls, struck us and went by, came back.

"A couple of kids," said the man holding the light. He sounded both disgusted and relieved. "Wouldn't you know."

The light shone steady in my eyes, making everything else black. The men were only dark figures behind it, which must have been their plan. They could see us, but we couldn't see them.

"Think we ought to call the cops?" asked the second man.

Call the cops, I thought. Please call the cops!

The first man hesitated, as if he might really call the police. "I don't know," he said. "Breaking and entering. They'd put these two away for a long time."

"No, don't," gasped Beaky, turning his head toward the light.

"Wow, look at that," said the first man.

"That has to be the ugliest girl God ever made," murmured his pal in shocked tones.

I slid my eyes sidewise at Beaky. He wasn't too attractive, with his big nose bright pink from his cold and his mouth hanging open to reveal his large teeth.

"What are you two doing here in the middle of the night?"

"Yeah," said the other man. "What are you kids up

to in this nice, dry carpeted place?" And they both laughed.

"Want your momma to find out, girlie?"

Beaky shook his head.

Beaky might be numb with shock or fright, but my temper was starting to take over. These men actually thought that Beaky was a girl and that I was with him! The rest of what they thought, I didn't even want to imagine. I wanted to yell at them, to snatch Beaky's hat off his head and show he was a guy, but I didn't. I bit my tongue till it bled.

"Look at the little guy," said the man with the light. "Poor little fella's embarrassed."

"Let us alone," I said. My voice sounded high-pitched and frightened, not at all angry.

The man took a step forward.

Beaky buried his face in my right shoulder and hung on to me harder. I staggered under the additional weight.

"Cut it out," said the other man. "Can't you see you're scaring his girl?"

I almost threw up. Instead I closed my eyes tightly, as if somehow that would make me invisible.

"Think we ought to turn them in?"

"Naw. Give the kid a break. Anyone with a girl-friend that ugly has enough problems."

"You mean you're going to let us go?" choked out Beaky.

"Yeah. This time. You go on out the front way and don't you look back. You run and keep running, and don't ever come back here again. You do, and we'll call the police."

"Or else we'll take care of you ourselves," said the

man with the light. The tone of his voice made it very clear that if they took care of us themselves, there wouldn't be much left.

Beaky and I did as we were told. We went out the front entrance and we ran. I don't know where Beaky ran—home I guess, the long tan raincoat flapping around his legs and the brimmed hat flying in the wind.

As for me, I didn't slow down until I was in my front yard. By the side of the house, I doubled over, my legs cramped and my chest heaving for air.

"Don't ever come back here," the man had said.

We'll see, I told myself grimly. Before that night, the whole adventure had been sort of pretend, sneaking out with Beaky and hiding in the bushes and acting as if we were big-deal crime catchers. Now something personal had entered it. Those men had insulted and threatened me, Scott Pritchard. I wanted them to pay for that.

8

"I wasn't scared" was the first thing Beaky said when he saw me at ball practice the next night. "I've been studying acting for a long time, three or four years, and I thought that would be a good act to help us to escape."

"Where are you studying acting?" I didn't think there would be much use for Beaky in films except in monster movies.

"On my own," he said, his cow eyes defensive. "I watch all the TV I can, and I read up on actors in the library. I wasn't scared one little bit."

"That's good, because we're going back there."

"We are?" His voice went high.

"Yeah. Those guys humiliated us. We got to get even."

"But Scott—"

I fixed him with a long, level stare, cool and determined.

"Okay," he said. "But I can't tonight. I have to get my sleep. I have a test in language arts tomorrow, and I'm failing this term."

Details. I shrugged. I couldn't care less if Beaky failed all his subjects. They'd hold him back, and then I wouldn't be faced with having him in any of my classes.

"Let's gue. Let's gue," shouted Coach Bob Baker, waving at the two of us, motioning us over to where the rest of the team was gathering into a ragged line. This was the day for our team picture. We were wearing our uniforms for the first time.

Pretending to tie my shoe, I held back so that I didn't have to stand near Beaky in the picture. I know I'm not short, but sometimes I feel like a runt. Anyone next to Beaky was going to look like a dwarf.

When I straightened, I stood for a couple of seconds, looking at the coaches and the team. Bob Baker was trying to arrange the guys in some sort of order. Mr. Mathais was watching, scratching at the bald spot on his head as usual, looking as if he were trying to think. The photographer was adjusting his camera, moving forward, backing up.

When I think of a baseball team, I think of a gang of kids all about the same height, not tall, not short, sturdy-looking. They are dressed exactly alike, in neat white uniforms with the name of their team in navy blue script across the back. The kids are wearing navy blue socks with their individual numbers in white on the legs. They look very serious, like an efficient machine, ready to win games.

Lyttons' Losers didn't look at all like that. Oh, we had the white uniforms with the team name all right, and our socks were navy blue and we had the numbers on them, but that is where the resemblance to a real baseball team ended. The guys on Lyttons' were all different sizes, some tall and some short. A couple were so skinny I doubted they ate more than one meal a day, and one was so fat he could practically roll around the bases. Some of them didn't look older than ten, and there were two who needed to shave at least twice a week but didn't bother.

"Come on, Pritchard!" yelled Coach Bob Baker.

I sauntered over and joined the group, trying to hide myself in the back behind a big kid, Chris Singleton.

"Stand in front of Singleton, Pritchard," said Mr. Mathais. He stopped scratching his bald spot long enough to point. "And Singleton. Tuck in that shirt."

There were a few stray laughs, because Mr. Mathais' shirttail always hung out one side or the other, but no one dared say anything. Coach Bob Baker might seem as if he were in charge of Lyttons', but we'd all found out fast that Mr. Mathais really was.

Mr. Mathais squinted. "All right. Norton, you come out in the center and pretend you are making a catch. Shawn, you stand on one side of Norton. Harris, you stand on the other."

Beaky squatted and held his mitt out in front of him. From my angle, his legs stuck up and his elbows jutted out and his head poked forward. If he'd been wearing a green uniform, we wouldn't have been able to tell him from a giant grasshopper.

On one side of Beaky, Shawn stood very tall, which

brought the top of his head about four inches above the top of Beaky's. Harris, on the other side, wasn't so lucky. Harris will never make five feet if he lives to be one hundred, and they stretch him. He is the smallest kid I know, even counting the girls. He is also one of the best players on Lyttons'.

Our coaches conferred. Then they walked over to one end of the back row and stood ready for the picture. No one told Mr. Mathais that his shirttail was hanging out. No one told Beaky his baseball cap was pulled down so far that his nose looked like it had a roof over it. No one said anything while the photographer took our picture.

We looked exactly like what we were—a bunch of losers.

After the team picture, we broke up into orange and navy to play. The field was still soggy from all the rain the night before. Our new uniforms were plastered with mud almost immediately, which made us look a little more professional. It also made both the ball and the bat harder to hold on to, although the batboy kept drying them both on an old towel.

The guys were in high spirits. They went slipping and sliding through the mud, hooting and hollering and missing the ball, and nobody seemed to care. Even the coaches didn't much care, which was very unusual, since they're always yelling about good discipline and lots of effort.

Most days I would have joined in the fun. I like sliding in the mud and hollering myself. But that evening I didn't feel up to it. I hadn't slept at all after we had been caught by the men, not during the night, not during school. Between that and trying to control my temper, and realizing that my team looked like a bunch of rejects, I wasn't in a very good mood.

I struck out my first time at bat. Beaky didn't say anything about it. He looked as tired as I felt, dark circles under his dark eyes, his nose pink and running from his cold. He also blinked constantly, as if the bright sunlight hurt his eyes.

In the fourth inning, I missed an easy catch at third base, and the guy on second went for home. Then Shawn flubbed the ball in the outfield, and the kid who got it slipped in the mud. Orange made two runs off my mistake.

"Way to go, Ape Ears," shouted one of their men from the bench, trying to get under my skin.

I would have liked to kill him. Instead, I calmly looked back toward home plate, remembering what Dr. Wocoviak had told me about trying to analyze a situation and control it. I watched as Norris caught a long fly to the outfield to retire the side.

"You blew it, Ape Ears," said our pitcher, Chris Singleton, as I passed him on the way toward the bench. He slapped me hard on the butt.

I ignored him, but as I walked toward the bench, I settled my baseball cap a little higher on my head so it didn't rest on my ears.

Beaky was already into a deep squat, catching for the orange team's pitcher, who was warming up. Beaky was getting a whole lot better at catching. I bet Rutledge Rims will be sorry that they overlooked old Beaky. Sometimes talent is a little hard to spot when it comes in a strange package.

I dropped onto the bench at a place where there was

a tree I could lean back against. I leaned, pulled my hat down so my eyes were deeply shaded, and closed them. Within seconds, I was asleep.

"Pritchard!"

"Unh. Hunh?" I came awake and almost fell off the bench.

"Move it! Is practice so boring you can't keep your eyes open?" Bob Baker sounded mad. I guess he was tired of all the horsing around.

"I'm awake. I'm awake."

"You could have fooled me out there on third."

I turned, ready to argue, then shut my mouth. He was right. I had been practically asleep on third base.

I shuffled over to the batter's box and picked up the bat. It was cold and damp, almost wet. I gripped it and tried a few experimental swings. Then I took my place next to the plate and waited for the pitch.

It came in low and wide.

"Strike one!" called Bob Baker.

"That was a ball!" I protested, turning toward him.

"It was a strike," he said quietly.

Fuming, I faced the pitcher, shifting my feet in the sticky mud, wiggling my rear end.

I swung and missed.

"Hey, Ape Ears, can't you see?" yelled their second baseman. A guy on our bench hooted.

It took a long time until the next pitch. Their pitcher seemed to look at Beaky forever. I didn't know what Beaky was doing behind me, what signal he was giving, if he was giving any signal at all. I guessed that he was only delaying, trying to make me nervous so I would strike out.

I breathed deeply.

The bat connected. I could tell from the feel that it wasn't a good hit, but it was all I had. I raced toward first, seeing from the corner of my left eye the pitcher scrambling for the ball, throwing toward base.

The first baseman stepped in front of the bag and pushed his body toward me, deflecting me. I went down into the mud.

I bounced to my feet immediately, but he held the ball.

"He's blocking the bag!" I screamed. "That's illegal!"

All of navy came off the bench. The guys on orange left their positions, edging closer.

"You shoved me!" I thrust my face into the face of the first baseman.

"I did not," he yelled, his feet planted firmly in the mud, one fist holding out the ball for me to see. "I had the ball all the time. It was a fair out."

"Was not!"

"Was too!"

"Get him, Ape Ears," somebody yelled from my team.

"Prissy Pritchard," yelled someone from orange.

I looked at the coaches. They were there all right, watching, but not interfering.

"Cheater!" I yelled.

"Ah, blow it out your ear!"

At that point, the coaches moved between us. They talked for a couple of minutes to both of us, but I didn't hear a word. Finally they stopped talking, and it was mostly silent on the field.

"What was the call?" asked the pitcher for orange.

"Out," said Bob Baker.

"You lose, Prissy," said their first baseman.

I went berserk. I tore the cap off my head and threw it in the mud and screamed and yelled. I screamed a lot of stuff about a bunch of losers and about dumb coaches and about how I hated all of them and baseball too. I kicked at the mud and swung my arms and let out frantic shrieks.

Then I stopped.

Everyone on Lyttons Union Co-op was staring at me —the boys, the coaches, even the little kid who acted as batboy. They all stood and looked at me as if I were some sort of weird circus animal that they had never seen before. I looked toward the parking area where the mothers were waiting. They were staring too.

"I quit," I said hoarsely.

Neither coach said a word. Mr. Mathais leaned over and picked my hat out of the mud and handed it to me. Then everyone watched as I turned and walked off the field.

9

Like the sound of a record stuck in a groove, the sound of my shrieks and yells kept repeating in my head, and that was the best part. The worst part was the way I kept seeing the scene again and again like in a movie, only now I saw it from the viewpoint of the coaches and the other players. I had made a fool of myself.

I didn't need any counselor to tell me to analyze what had happened and what I had gained or lost from it. I knew what I had lost. I had lost my place on the baseball team and I had lost my self-respect. I didn't even try to tell myself that it was all right, that I'd had to defend myself and my reputation. This time I knew better. I knew exactly what I had done, and I felt like the world's worst jerk for doing it.

After that, I didn't need anyone to explain why my

parents thought I needed a counselor. For the first time, I was perfectly willing to admit that my temper was getting me nowhere, zilch, nothing. All it was doing was wrecking my life. The problem was that making the lists and analyzing what was happening didn't seem to help much.

Dr. Wocoviak listened while I told him about throwing my cap down and kicking and screaming and quitting the team. He didn't seem as impressed by all that as I was. I guess he has probably seen a lot worse things.

He did get me to talk some more, about my feelings about school and my family and the baseball team. School and the family weren't much. They were both okay, except that bratty Tina was still calling me Teenybopper. I kept going back to baseball and talking about that. Finally, as I had about run out of things to say, I thought of something else.

"If my grandfather marries Beaky Norton's grandmother," I asked, "will Beaky and I be related?"

"What?" He began to smile.

"Will we be like cousins or something?"

"Well, I don't know about the legal sense—"

"That's okay. I was just wondering." Somehow being related to Beaky didn't seem as horrible a prospect as it would have a month ago. In one way, I could be grateful to him and his grandmother. Mrs. Norton and my grandpa were off somewhere, drinking coffee and eating doughnuts, so Grandpa missed my big fit on the baseball field.

"Don't you like Beaky's grandmother?"

"She's okay, but I don't like her hanging around the baseball field. Lots of times when she drops Beaky off, she stands there and watches, and she doesn't go way off to one side the way the mothers do. She stands real close where she can hear every little thing."

"What's wrong with that?"

"Well, she's a grandmother! You know. We can't even talk regular with her around."

"You mean you can't use foul language?"

Foul language—that sounded like something a man who wore ties with fish on them would say, I thought. Out loud, I said, "She calls Beaky *Stanley* and she's always asking dumb questions. How can a guy think about baseball when there's an old lady hanging around asking dumb questions?"

"So Beaky Norton's grandmother is the reason you quit the team?"

"No." I felt a little disappointed that he could think I was trying to make excuses. "The reason I quit the team was that I got mad and lost my temper and said a bunch of things I didn't mean."

"Man," I added, "I embarrassed myself so bad I don't know if I could ever go back there and look all those guys in the face." I glanced at Dr. Wocoviak, half hoping he'd have some good advice.

"That's something you'll have to work on" was all he said.

That was what he usually said, I thought sourly. My parents had to go and hire a counselor who didn't do half the work he was paid for. Instead, he expected me to solve my problems myself.

"Guess this is it for today," said Dr. Wocoviak, shoving his chair backward, the casters squealing. "I have to check on the rats."

"Rats?"

"Yep, rats. I hired a new lab assistant, but she has to finish another job before she can start here, so I've been taking care of them all week."

"I thought you already got a new assistant." I stood as he did, watching him pat his shirt pockets. Dr. Wocoviak looked as if he were feeding himself a lot more than he was feeding the rats. He was getting a big belly.

"I had to let her go." He stretched. "She was a good worker, did everything she was supposed to—" He hesitated, looking at me as if he had just thought of something. "Want to come along?"

"Sure." I didn't have anything better to do. It was going to be a long evening. All the other guys would be practicing baseball, and I would be home the same as the last three nights. "Why'd you get rid of her then?" I asked as I followed him through a door and down a green-painted hall.

"She didn't like rats," he said, pushing open a door at the end of the corridor. "Rats need someone who cares about them."

We entered a small room that smelled sort of like a doctor's office. Along one wall were two long tables with white Formica tops. Over to one side, under a bank of windows, were several cupboards and a big wooden box up on one end. The inside floor of the box was painted in white and black checks.

On the opposite side of the room, against an inside wall, were a lot of little cages, maybe twenty or thirty. Each one held a rat.

When we entered the room, some of the rats came to the front of their cages to look at us. Several stood on their hind feet, their noses sniffing at the heavy wire mesh separating them from the outside world. I stared at them, and they stared back. I moved a little closer.

"They're sleepy," said Dr. Wocoviak. "For a rat, late afternoon is just before dawn." He pulled one of the cages out like a drawer and carried it to the Formica tabletop. I followed him, looking down through the opening.

The rat inside was much smaller than I had expected. It was mostly white with a slatey gray head and some gray spots down its back. It put its front feet on the top edge of the cage and stretched up, staring at me through dark intelligent eyes.

Dr. Wocoviak picked the rat up and let it run over his folded arms. I put out one finger and touched its head. The fur was soft and warm and silky.

"I never knew rats were this nice," I said.

"These are Long-Evans hooded rats," said Dr. Wocoviak. "Some labs use albinos, but I got used to these fellows as a graduate student and I've never ordered anything else." He put the rat back in its cage and the cage back in its slot. "I knew a guy once who kept one as a pet. He said it was the best friend he had."

I laughed.

"What's funny?"

"My dumb little sister's birthday is in two weeks. Maybe I could give her a rat." Tina always wanted a pet. A rat would be perfect, I thought, eyeing them.

Dr. Wocoviak nodded. He was getting out animal food, but I didn't watch him. I was too busy studying the rats. Some were making soft, squeaking noises. I looked at the little tags fastened to the outsides of the cages and moved closer to read them.

"Jupiter," I read out loud. "Big Momma, Sam. They have names!"

"Of course," he said. "Some of them seem to recognize their names. At least the students insist they do."

"You," I said, and gulped, "perform experiments on these rats?" I imagined a little operating theater, Dr. Wocoviak in a green mask and gown, a pretty girl student handing him a scalpel, and a small furry body waiting to be cut open. I hoped he put them to sleep first.

"Psychology experiments," he said. "Look." He picked up a little whistle and blew. All the rats ran to the left sides of their cages and waited, their eyes shining.

"Why'd they do that?"

"The rats have learned that when a whistle blows, they are going to be fed on the left side of the cage, so that's where they go. A man named Pavlov once taught dogs to salivate at the sound of a bell. That's called a conditioned reflex."

"Oh."

"Most of our experiments with these rats have to do with studies about response."

I watched him as he put food pellets in the cages and checked water bottles. None of the rats tried to escape, but a couple butted their heads against his fingers when he reached into their cages. Maybe he wasn't fooling about their liking someone who cared about them.

"Suppose I didn't feed them when the whistle blew," he said. "What do you think would happen? Would they still run to the left side of the cage when I blew it?"

"No. Not after a while."

"Exactly." He stopped what he was doing for a moment and stared at me with his look that was like a hypnotist's.

Dr. Wocoviak didn't say much else. He went on feeding the rats, and I helped him. He didn't need to say anything else. I wasn't dumb. I knew my famous Pritchard temper reaction was a lot like the rats' reaction to the whistle.

What if instead of getting mad every time I thought someone was teasing me, I stayed cool? Maybe it wouldn't work at first, and maybe it wouldn't work at all, but it was worth trying. It had to be better than what was happening now—holding my anger deep inside where it simmered and boiled and made my stomach hurt and finally caused me to blow my top the way I had at baseball practice. Instead of feeding my anger when I felt it growing, I could try to go the other way, try harder to control my temper and analyze, like Dr. Wocoviak said.

That night I thought a lot about keeping cool, and I thought about how soft the fur of the rat had felt. I wondered if I bought Tina a rat for her birthday whether it would bite her or she would bite it. If I got her one, maybe she would let me hold it and feed it sometimes. Thinking about that made me feel better.

10

The next few days were exactly like the last ones, long and boring with plenty of time to think about baseball and my temper and rats. My mother washed my baseball uniform, and Grandpa took it over to the field to give it back to the coaches. He still went to practice every day to see Beaky's grandmother. He also took her out lots on dates to dinner and the movies and other places. These days when Grandpa stopped by our house, he was always smiling.

I felt particularly depressed on Saturday when Lyttons' had a practice game with another team in the league. Shawn came over afterward and told me all about it.

"We tied" were the first words he spoke.

"Tied?" I gaped at him like an idiot.

"Yeah. Norris hit a home run, and I singled twice."

He twitched his nose, his eyes sparkling behind his wire rims. "We have another game lined up for next Saturday, a team in some other league."

All of this made me feel very sad and left out. Shawn must have noticed, because after he told me some more about the practice game, he said very casually, "Why don't you come to the game next Saturday?"

"No."

"I bet if you asked, you could be back on the team. Mr. Mathais said he was holding your uniform."

At the thought of facing Mr. Mathais, I shuddered. Shawn said he understood, but it was clear he didn't. He told me a bunch of the guys said hi, and then I told him I was going to see a counselor about my temper. Shawn didn't seem very much surprised. He said that he had noticed that I was able to take some teasing now without punching out anybody's lights.

Then he told me that Beaky Norton got a moped that he sometimes rode to practice.

"He carries his catcher's mitt in a bowling bag," said Shawn. "He gave me a ride home the other night, and it was great. Oh, he said to tell you he would call you when things looked right. What did he mean by that?"

"I'm not sure," I hedged.

Another two days crawled by. I went to school and got my sleep at night and thought about baseball. Finally, I told Shawn I would go to the game Saturday.

I was so bored and lonely all week that when Beaky called at last, I felt as if he were an old friend. I was so enthusiastic that at first Beaky thought he had the wrong number.

We met at his house at midnight, and we went

through the trees to check the condominiums. There was no sign of the men.

"I'm sure they'll come tonight," said Beaky. "A big shipment of televisions arrived today. I bet they could sell stolen televisions real easy."

"At least it isn't raining," I said cheerfully. "Beaky, old boy, I heard that you got a moped. How about letting me look at it while we wait for them to show up?"

Beaky went for the suggestion the way the trout went for the fly on Dr. Wocoviak's tie. He even rolled the thing out of his garage and into the moonlight so I could have a better view.

I whistled softly. It was one fine moped, all the gadgets, a lot of chrome. I ran one hand over the seat. Two of us could squeeze on there easily.

"Your parents rich or something?" I asked.

"No. I'm just spoiled."

I laughed and punched him lightly on the shoulder. "How 'bout a ride?"

"Sure. Come on over tomorrow after school."

"I mean right now."

"We can't. Mopeds aren't allowed on the street after nine o'clock in the evening," said Beaky. "City ordinance 404."

"How would your parents like to know that their precious son has been sneaking out of the house in the middle of the night?" I asked pleasantly.

I think Beaky turned green. I'm not certain because colors look a lot alike in the moonlight.

"Okay," he said weakly, "but only a short one."

That wasn't exactly what I had in mind, and I told him so. Then we spent about fifteen minutes arguing.

As usual, I won. When we stalked through the trees to look for the thieves, Beaky had agreed to follow their van on his moped when it left the condominiums.

The men had arrived while we were arguing and were busily stowing televisions in the back of the van. Beaky and I sneaked back into the trees, then across his lawn to his garage. We wheeled the moped out of the garage, down the sidewalk, and around the block. We hid in an alley south of the condominiums. The men had turned in this direction before; I was trusting fate that they would again.

We couldn't have been in place very long when we heard the low sound of a motor and saw a dark shape in the moonlight moving toward us. As the van came even with us, the headlights flashed on.

"Let's move!" I said, hopping onto the back of the moped.

"I have to put my helmet on." Beaky took a huge white helmet off the handlebars and put it over his head, starting to fasten the straps.

"We'll lose them!"

"I promised my mom I would always wear a safety helmet when I rode my moped."

I stifled a groan. I was certain we would lose them. The van wasn't going very fast, but a moped is really slow.

The moped wasn't all that slow once Beaky got it going, but we would have lost the van anyway if it hadn't stopped at a light at the corner of Morrison and Fulton. As soon as he spotted the red light and the van's taillights, Beaky pulled up on the sidewalk into the shadow of a building and stopped too.

"I still think I should put on my headlight," he whispered.

"You want those men to look in the rearview mirror and see us?" I was already worried about the noise, but Beaky's moped was very quiet.

Beaky shut up. We waited silently, staring at the van.

The red light seemed to last forever. Not another vehicle passed while we waited, not a car or a truck or anything. The van sat all alone at that light in the middle of the night, waiting, while Beaky and I waited several hundred yards behind. I wondered if the men in the van were as nervous as I was.

At last the light flashed green, and the van moved off, Beaky and I following like a toy on a string.

We must have trailed them for miles. I tried to keep a record of the blocks, but I lost track. I did figure out that we were headed through the north end of town. I only hoped the men weren't going too far. I didn't know how much gasoline Beaky had.

While some small part of my brain worried at that, the rest was keenly aware of the wind in my hair, the trees and lights and darkened buildings flashing by, and the tense excitement in Beaky's body as he hunched forward over the handlebars. There was the steady throb of the machine beneath me, the low sound of its motor and the surge of pure pleasure at hurtling through the deserted streets.

Just when I was beginning to want our wild ride to last forever, the van passed an abandoned Kroger supermarket and picked up speed. Our moped began to fall behind.

"Faster!" I shouted into Beaky's ear.

"It won't go any faster!"

He tried. He kept the moped flat out, but after another four blocks, the van made a left turn at an elementary school and we lost them.

Beaky turned onto the school playground and killed the engine. He crawled off the moped, and I did too.

"No use." He looked down the street. In the distance, taillights glimmered faintly and were gone.

"If you hadn't been messing with that stupid helmet—"

"Hey! We caught up with them after that." Beaky yawned and stretched.

"Now we'll have to do it all over again another night."

"What?" He dropped his arms. "No way."

Our voices must have been getting louder and louder, but I guess neither of us noticed. We argued a few more minutes over what we should do about the men. Beaky wanted to forget all about them or call the police, and I wanted to continue our stakeout and follow them another night.

"You're going to get us into all kinds of trouble," protested Beaky.

"Listen, Stanley," I began.

BLAM!

One minute I was on my feet, arguing with Beaky, the next I was flat on my back, staring at the stars. They were moving in a lazy circle far above me.

"You hit me," I said in amazement.

"Stand up and fight!" roared Beaky.

"But you hit me." I sat up, still dazed.

"Prepare to defend yourself."

"But why? What did I do?" I was so astonished, I didn't get mad. I didn't even *think* of getting mad.

"You called me a name."

"I only called you—"

"Don't say it!"

Across the street from the playground, a window was thrown up. "Shut up out there," a man screamed. "It's two o'clock in the morning!"

"I never knew you would hit someone," I said, lowering my voice. I climbed to my hands and knees and then to my feet.

"Everyone has their breaking point," said Beaky very loudly.

"If you kids don't shut up, I'm calling the cops!"

Beaky ignored him. Instead he clenched his hands into fists and made threatening gestures toward me.

"Apologize," he demanded.

"I apologize," I whispered. I climbed back onto the moped, a wary eye cocked toward the man across the street. He was leaning out the window, his head thrust our direction. When he saw me looking, he shook his fist.

"Promise me you'll never say it again."

"I promise."

Beaky considered, his back stiff, his eyes glittering in the moonlight. As he climbed back onto the moped, the man disappeared from the window.

"If we follow those men another night," said Beaky, pressing his advantage, turning his key in the ignition, "we'll only lose them again."

"Don't worry about it," I mumbled. "I have a plan."

11

I suppose I should have been nervous about facing the coaches and the team on Saturday, but I wasn't. I had so many other things on my mind that I barely gave the practice game a thought.

One evening after school I took my bicycle and rode over to the north end of town. It took me over an hour, but I finally located the abandoned Kroger store. After that, it was easy. Another ten minutes and I was sitting on my bicycle on the school playground, surveying the area.

It wasn't as beat-up by day as it had looked by night. As a matter of fact, most of the neighborhood was nice in a run-down sort of way. The playground was well taken care of, the shrubs trimmed, and the equipment painted. There were ruts in the grass from hundreds of kids' feet and some initials carved in the only tree that had survived years of schoolkids hanging on it, but it was as decent as any playground I'd ever seen.

It was the houses in the area that interested me. Some of them were pretty small, although there were several that were big old duplexes. There were houses with broken windows patched with tape and rusty broken-out screens, the yards weedy and littered, but there were also lots of houses that were well taken care of, especially the front yards. There were plenty of daffodils and tulips blooming, more than on our block, and one yard had a whole collection of fake animals and people. There were Snow White and the Seven Dwarfs, and two miniature deer, and a white enameled cat on the porch roof. There was also a creature looking out of a bush near the front steps. I couldn't tell if it was a gnome or a monkey or something else. I considered crossing the street to get a better look, but I didn't want anyone to notice me nosing around.

Next door to that house, directly across from the playground, was the house where the big man had leaned out the second-story window. It was painted a dark shiny green. In front of every window in the whole house was a matching green window box filled with red flowers that looked like geraniums. Since it was too early for real geraniums, I figured they had to be fake ones. The whole effect reminded me of Christmas, but the man who lived there sure didn't act like one of Santa's helpers. Before he could spot me and recognize me as one of the kids who woke him up at two in the morning, I hopped back on my bike and got out of there.

Another day after school, I walked to the pet store up on Stark Street. The store had only one rat in stock, an albino, but it was a very large handsome creature who wiped at its immaculate whiskers with one paw and stared at me out of shiny pink eyes. It cost more than I wanted to spend, but it was worth it. I figured Tina wasn't the only one who was going to enjoy the rat. The whole family would like it, especially me.

The rat was a girl rat, but the man behind the counter assured me that I wouldn't be getting any babies for free. He also tried to sell me a cage, but I decided the cage we had leftover from my rabbit who died would be perfect. Besides, I had only enough money with me to buy the rat and food for a couple weeks. Tina's birthday was in six days. She could buy her own rat food after that.

I took the rat home and hid it in a ten-gallon aquarium in the back of my closet. The aquarium was bigger than Dr. Wocoviak's cages, and besides, I thought Mom might get suspicious if she saw me dragging the rabbit cage up to my room. While I did all this, I made plans to buy myself a boy rat.

Grandpa and Mrs. Norton drove Shawn and Beaky and me to the game on Saturday. I felt a little funny, sitting in the car in regular clothes with Shawn and Beaky in their uniforms, but I didn't let it throw me.

The guys on the other team were huge and tough-looking, big enough to play for some high school and mean enough to be in a gang of street fighters instead of members of a kids' baseball team. They hiccoughed and belched and made coarse gestures when they saw us, and their coaches didn't say one little thing about it. I think maybe their coaches were afraid of them.

When Mr. Mathais told me I could sit on the bench with the rest of the guys, I wondered why. I looked at

74

Shawn, but he was pitching the ball at Norris and didn't see me. Nobody paid much attention to me. A couple of the guys said hi, but mostly they seemed to be staring at the other team.

My grandpa and Mrs. Norton weren't the only relatives at the game. A lot of mothers were there too, and some fathers and a herd of younger brothers and sisters. They stood around yakking and calling to each other and then finally climbed onto the rickety old bleachers behind our team's bench, but they didn't shut up. They seemed a lot more interested in talking to each other than they did in watching the game.

It was a good thing it was only a practice game. From the very beginning, it was clear that we were losers all right. I guess it was a good experience to prepare us for the regular season.

I sat and watched and was almost glad I didn't have to play—almost. The other team acted as if every little thing was a big deal. They argued over every call that went against them, and they played mean and rough. Also, they laughed and made fun of our team the whole time they were playing.

For me, the game was sort of interesting, mostly because I wasn't involved. I could sit on the bench and watch and not take anything personally, although I did feel a little bit angry when one of their batters gave Beaky a push on his back as Beaky passed. Beaky fell over on his face in the dirt by home plate. The guy laughed and swung his bat over Beaky's back. The umpire didn't do a single thing about it.

I looked at Bob Baker and Mr. Mathais. Bob Baker was pacing nervously, his wiry body tense. Mr. Mathais wasn't scratching at his bald spot. He was staring at the other team's coaches and shaking his head in disgust. When Beaky was shoved and the umpire did nothing, Mr. Mathais called Bob Baker to him. They conferred for a couple of minutes. Then Mr. Mathais went over and said something to Beaky.

At the end of the second inning, the other team had fifteen runs and we had zip.

"How do you like the score?" I asked Chris Singleton, our pitcher. What I really wanted to say was "You blew it," the way Chris had the day I got mad and quit the team, but I didn't.

"I just want to get out of here in one piece," said Chris. This surprised me because Chris is a big guy who's never even been afraid of the famous Pritchard temper.

Right after Chris said that, I became aware of something. The people behind me on the bleachers had shut up. There wasn't a single sound coming from them. I turned around on the bench to look at them.

They were staring at the field, and they weren't happy. Some of them looked disgusted, and a couple of the mothers, Norris' for example, looked worried. It was a bright sunny day, and they should have been having a good time watching their boys play a practice game, but instead they seemed angry or depressed.

The game continued. The other team scored eight more runs. When our side came up in the fourth, we did manage to get two hits and two men on base with no outs. Then Shawn came up to bat.

"Rah, Shawn," shouted Norris, stamping his feet in the dirt. Some of the other guys did the same. I whistled.

Shawn is not a very good hitter. All of us on the

bench knew he was going to strike out; we would have bet money on it. The pitcher on the other team didn't know that though. He squinted at us on the bench, then he squinted at Shawn.

He must have decided that Shawn was our best hitter and that our team was finally going to get a run in. He wiggled his shoulders and shuffled his feet. Then he threw the ball straight at Shawn's head.

Shawn ducked.

The pitcher smiled. He stretched his arms over his head and threw the ball straight at Shawn again.

Shawn jumped back.

"Strike!" called the umpire.

From behind me on the bleachers came a low rumbling sound like a growl. Coach Bob Baker ran over to where the umpire was and started talking at him fast, pointing at the pitcher and at Shawn and waving his arms around. Mr. Mathais followed Bob Baker slowly. The three of them called the pitcher to them. The other team's coaches came too.

They talked.

We waited.

The sun was hot. I stretched my arms and thought about ways I could tell our coaches I was sorry I had made a fool of myself and ask if I could be back on the team.

Finally the huddle broke up. Our coaches walked back toward our bench, looking very serious and a little disgruntled. The other team's pitcher went back to the pitcher's mound, a big fat grin on his face. The umpire took his place behind the plate.

Bob Baker and Mr. Mathais were talking together, watching the pitcher. Shawn picked up the bat and took a couple of swings. It took courage to go back into the batting box, but he did it.

The pitcher looked at Shawn, looked at our coaches, looked at the umpire. He smiled. Then he pursed his lips and hawked a big glob of spit right on the ball. He rubbed it in with his hands.

"Wait a minute!" It was the first time I ever heard Mr. Mathais raise his voice. He waved Shawn out of the batter's box as he headed toward the pitcher's mound.

"You hawked on the ball!"

"So what?" sneered the pitcher.

"That's a spitball. You can't do that!"

"Who says so?"

"*I* say so." Mr. Mathais thrust out his chin. It went almost as far out as his belly. "That's illegal."

"It isn't even sanitary!" yelled Bob Baker.

I glanced at the umpire. He was standing off to one side, his cap in his hands. He was studying the inside of the cap as if it held a map to buried treasure.

"I'm not going to hit that," said Shawn, not very loud, but loud enough for us on the bench to hear him.

"Hold on!" The coaches for the other team were coming, and a couple of their men left their positions. Behind me on the bleachers, some of the parents made catcalls. It wasn't very sporting, but then some parents aren't very good sports.

Out on the field, Bob Baker demanded that Shawn be walked to first, loading the bases, and that the pitcher be removed from the game.

One of their coaches was yelling at Bob Baker. The other one stood there with a silly smile on his face. The umpire watched from a safe distance. The expression on his face said that no job paid enough to have to deal with these maniacs.

Then the guys on our bench stood to get a better look at what was happening. Some of the other team started yelling things at us. We kept quiet. In a fair fight, they'd murder us, and the way they looked, not one would fight fair.

There was one of those sudden silences that sometimes happens in a lot of noise. Right in the middle of it, their pitcher said something really obscene.

"That's it!" shouted Bob Baker. "Let's gue." He waved an arm toward the bench and the bleachers. "We don't have to put up with this."

"Right!" yelled Norris' mother. That was all that was needed. In seconds, people were spilling off the bleachers, heading toward the side of the field where their cars were parked. Our team followed slowly, then more rapidly.

I looked back as we reached my grandfather's car. The other team was still standing on the field. They didn't look tough anymore. They only looked dumbfounded.

About halfway home, Shawn observed, "This was our second game, and we still didn't get a chance to do our team cheer."

"We'll probably never get the chance to do it," said Beaky. He sat slouched on the back seat between Shawn and me, his long arms and legs crammed into the small space.

"Come on, you guys. Cheer up," said Grandpa. "Tell you what. We have lots of time. Let's stop at Friendly's for a snack."

It was a great idea. Grandpa settled us boys in a booth and told us to order whatever we wanted. He and Mrs. Norton sat across the aisle, talking quietly.

Beaky and Shawn and I got pretty loud, so loud that the man behind the counter kept glaring at us; but Grandpa and Mrs. Norton didn't seem to notice our noise at all. They were only interested in each other.

Partway through my hot fudge sundae, it occurred to me that my grandpa didn't have a problem anymore. He didn't even need a counselor to help solve it. All Grandpa needed was Beaky's grandmother.

12

When I had my appointment with Dr. Wocoviak, I told him all about the baseball game and what happened. I told him that I had bought Tina a rat for her birthday and that I had made an A on my social studies paper. I didn't mention that the condominiums had received another shipment of televisions and that Beaky and I planned to catch the criminals that night, but I did talk about what took place between Shawn and me. That was the most important event that had happened to me in a long time.

I had gone over to Shawn's house Sunday afternoon. Mostly I went there because it was what I did nearly every Sunday afternoon of my life, but also because I wanted to tell him about Beaky and me following those men. I figured someone should know about it in case anything happened to us. But I sure didn't want to tell my parents. As it worked out though, I didn't mention Beaky or the men.

Shawn has been my best friend ever since kindergarten. That was a long time ago, but I still remember the first day I met him. A big first grader was threatening to mash me to a pulp on the playground, and Shawn stepped in and told him to can it. That's exactly what he said, "Can it." Of course Shawn was a lot bigger then, I mean in relation to the other kids. He was the biggest kid in my kindergarten class, and I was the smallest. From then on, he was my hero.

As the years went by, I grew and grew, and Shawn only grew a little bit. Pretty soon I was taller than he was by an inch and then by a full head. I was bigger, but Shawn was still my hero.

I wasn't thinking about all that on Sunday. I was only thinking about how I could tell Shawn about Beaky and me and our nights out without hurting his feelings. I didn't want him to think that I would prefer to hang out with Beaky Norton instead of him.

There were a lot of kids around Shawn's house, as usual. He has three sisters and a brother who is a senior in high school, so there is always a mob scene with all their friends and with Mr. and Mrs. Davis too. Shawn and I went out to the garage and tossed a deflated basketball toward a rusty old hoop that hung there.

Shawn flipped the ball toward the basket with one hand. It hit the rim of the hoop and fell to the ground with a dull thud. Neither Shawn nor I moved to pick it up. Basketball season was as far gone as the ball.

"You say anything to the coaches yet?" asked Shawn.

"About what?"

"About getting back on the team." He squinted at me, wrinkling his nose, which made his glasses rise.

"Not yet. I don't know what to tell them."

"That you're sorry and that you want back on the team." He was still looking at me, expectantly, like a rabbit.

I shifted uneasily and kicked at the basketball. It moved a couple of feet and stopped, settling into a misshapen sphere.

"Maybe it won't do any good."

"Sure it will."

"How do you know?"

Shawn sort of frowned. "I just know," he said.

He was holding back on me. Friends shouldn't hold back on each other. I was beginning to feel a little irritated, which surprised me. I am almost never irritated with Shawn.

"Did the tooth fairy tell you?" I asked sarcastically.

Shawn hesitated. "Mr. Mathais did," he mumbled.

"Tell you what?"

"That you could be back on the team if you talked to him about it."

For the first time in days, I felt the familiar heat of anger build in my arms, around the back of my neck. There was the compressed feeling in my chest and a tightness in my throat that usually signaled the onset of the Pritchard temper.

"You talked with Mr. Mathais about me?" I said, keeping my voice level. I looked steadily at my best friend. He really did resemble a rabbit, his nose twitching, his eyes alert behind his wire rims.

"I told him you were seeing a counselor about your temper."

"You what!"

"I only told *him*—"

"That's my business!" I yelled, advancing on him. How could he? "Now everyone will know about it."

"I'm sorry," said Shawn. He was very uneasy, but he didn't move away from me. His nose had stopped twitching. He stood very still, his eyes watching me, his arms dangling at his sides.

I wanted to hit him as much as I'd ever wanted to hit anyone in my life. I had trusted him with my secret, and he had told Mr. Mathais. If Mr. Mathais mentioned it to one kid, they'd all be laughing at me.

"Sure you're sorry," I snarled. I slit my eyes at Shawn. "And you are going to be sorrier."

Shawn inhaled sharply, then braced himself. He still didn't move away. He only watched me, his eyes steady and unafraid, waiting.

My body tensed. The muscles along the back of my shoulders lifted and bunched.

What will you get by hitting him? That thought popped into my head as I felt my hands curl into fists. What will you lose? Then I thought: Be cool, Scott. You don't *have* to hit him.

I took a deep breath, a second breath. Then I sort of shuddered. I licked my lips and shook my head. I stepped back a step. Putting a little distance between Shawn and me made me feel better, less like hitting him. I backed another step and took another deep breath.

I looked into Shawn's steady eyes, and I knew that it wasn't Shawn who was making me feel small and unimportant. The tension in my shoulders eased. I realized I wasn't going to hit him, and I felt enormously relieved.

"I guess you didn't mean anything by it," I said.

"I thought I might help," said Shawn. He was pale, but then Shawn is usually pale.

I nodded. Then I said, "I almost hit you."

"I'm glad you didn't."

"So am I." I was surprised. I didn't feel angry anymore, only relieved and a little shaky. It was a long way from not losing my temper at all, but it was a beginning.

"I'm especially glad because I decided a long time ago that if you ever beat up on me, we were finished as friends."

I jerked my head at him. His eyes behind his glasses were totally serious.

"Why?" I asked.

"Because I won't be beat on," said Shawn. "One time in the fifth grade, you hit Jason Holland for no reason at all—because he laughed at something you did that was funny."

"I did?" I couldn't remember.

"Yes. Right then, I decided that if you ever hit me, our friendship was off."

That really shook me. It wasn't as if I didn't have other friends, good friends like Beaky, but Shawn and I were like brothers. I didn't want anything to change that.

"Don't worry. I won't," I said.

"I know you won't," said Shawn.

It took almost my whole session with Dr. Wocoviak to tell him about my near fight with Shawn, about how I felt about it and how I figured out that I got mad at the teasing because I felt like some kind of runt, as if anyone who wanted could mess with me.

"And are you?"

"No," I said. "I used to be, a long time ago, in kindergarten."

"Does a runt have to hit people?"

"Shawn doesn't," I said, "and he is one of the littlest kids I know. I'm not going to either. I'm not going to be like a rat in a cage."

Dr. Wocoviak didn't say anything.

After a couple of seconds, I asked, "What about your rats? Don't you have to feed them?"

"No," said Dr. Wocoviak. "The new lab assistant likes rats."

"So do I."

"I have a meeting today, but if you want, next week we can take another look at them."

"Great."

"You are beginning to make progress, Scott," said Dr. Wocoviak.

Make progress. That sounded as if I had a long way to go, a lot of meetings with Dr. Wocoviak. That was okay. Maybe he could show me some experiments to do with Tina's girl rat, and my boy rat when I got him.

13

"What do you think about rats, Beaky?" I asked.

"As little as possible," said Beaky. It was 2:00 A.M., and we were on our stakeout at the elementary school playground. Beaky wasn't exactly pleased with the situation. I had the idea he'd prefer to go home and forget the whole thing.

"That's because you don't know any," I pointed out. "If you got to know a rat or two, you'd find out they are very interesting creatures."

Beaky yawned. Then he tried to shift his helmet back on his head and wipe under the front of it with his jacket sleeve. It was a warm night, the hottest we'd had so far this year, and his helmet wasn't helping much. I should know. Beaky had brought a helmet along for me and insisted that I wear it. He also insisted that we wear heavy jackets to protect us in case we fell. Thanks to the jackets and the helmets, we were steaming.

My helmet was candy-apple red, with flakes of gold sparkle through the paint. I poked an experimental finger up under the rim. My scalp was hot and sweaty. It was also very itchy.

"Where'd your mother get this helmet?" I asked, more to make conversation than because I wanted to know.

"At a garage sale."

"Whose garage sale?"

"I don't know. Some people's."

"You mean she didn't even know them?" All of a sudden, my scalp was itchier. I wondered if the helmet were full of fleas.

"Of course not. You don't have to know people to go to their stupid garage sales."

Or lice. It could be infested with lice. I had once seen a magnified picture of one. The thought of a louse living on my head, biting into me for a quick snack, was enough to make me gag. I fumbled at the strap under my chin.

"Leave it on," said Beaky.

"But it's hot."

"I said to leave it on," he repeated loudly. "If you drag me out here in the middle of the night, you wear the same equipment I do."

"Says who?" I yelled.

"If you want to ride on my moped, you wear it."

"SHUT UP OUT THERE!" This time we had no warning, no screech of a window flying up. It was warm out all right. The window must have already been open.

"Keep it on!" hissed Beaky. I know he thought he was keeping his voice down, but it resounded in the quiet night.

"You keep your traps closed, or I'll come down there and paste them shut!" the man yelled. Then he disappeared.

I don't know about Beaky, but to me the man sounded dangerous. I forgot all about the fleas and the head lice.

"Let's move down the block," I whispered to Beaky.

"Let's go home."

"We can go park where we saw the van's lights disappear."

"Is there any cover?"

"We can find some."

"Sure." It was plain he didn't believe me. "I'm staying right here or I'm going home."

"What about that man?"

"I'm a lot more afraid of those guys in the van spotting us than I am of an ordinary citizen."

"He doesn't seem like an ordinary citizen to me. How do we know he isn't some kind of maniac? He could specialize in dismembering young boys."

"If he was, he wouldn't have threatened to call the cops the other night."

"That's it. He only threatened," I said.

Beaky sighed and looked toward the sky. At least that was the direction the front of his white helmet turned.

"Norton, you are so dumb!" I exploded.

"It's not my fault we're out here in the middle of the night!"

Cree-onk. At first I thought it was some kind of an

animal cry. Then as I turned my head toward the house across the street, I recognized the sound. It was the noise nails make as they pull free of wood.

The big man was stretched out the window to get a better look at us. He was leaning on one of the green window boxes full of fake geraniums, but the window box wasn't strong enough to hold his weight. It was slowly pulling free from the house.

As I watched, the man made an acrobatic movement. It was clumsy, but he managed to save himself. The window box was not so lucky. One side of it hung several inches lower than before, at an angle to the window.

"OH, NO!" came a cry of despair. "FOR ONCE I GET A THING RIGHT, AND THEN SOME PUNKS COME ALONG IN THE MIDDLE OF THE NIGHT AND MAKE ME RUIN IT."

There was a bunch of mumbling, which I couldn't understand. Then a woman's voice said very clearly, "Harry, you come back to bed and leave those boys alone."

"THEY BUSTED MY WINDOW BOX! I'M GONNA BASH THEIR BRAINS IN! I'M GONNA TEAR OUT THEIR LIVERS!"

Beaky and I glanced at each other. We leaped toward his moped. I had my leg over the seat only seconds before he did. Beaky started it, or he tried to.

There was a series of crashing noises from inside the house. It could have been the sound of someone big falling down a flight of stairs.

"Hurry," I yelped at the back of the white helmet.

Beaky didn't answer. He was making frantic motions with his hands, kicking with his legs.

The door across the street slammed open. Framed in the opening was a huge man, big as a bear. In his right hand he carried something long and dark. It could have been a pipe or it could have been a wrench. I didn't want to find out which.

"Beaky," I whined.

"Harry!" yelled the woman from the bedroom window. "You come back here!"

Harry didn't listen. He charged down the sidewalk and across the street, making a sound that was a cross between screaming and grunting. He raised the black object high over his head as he came. It was the biggest wrench I'd ever seen.

I didn't realize that Beaky had the moped moving until we bumped into the street. Even so, it was very close. A few steps more, and Harry would have slaughtered us.

As it was, he made an Olympic effort at catching us, amazing for someone that big. He charged down the middle of the street behind us, swinging the wrench at the back of my head. I crouched low, trying to bury my head in Beaky's back, grateful that his mom had bought the helmet, fleas and lice or not.

It must have been three hundred yards before I no longer heard a grunting in my ears or the whistle of a large hard object passing directly behind me. It was another half block before I dared to raise my head to take a look over my shoulder.

Harry was still coming. He couldn't have been more than two car lengths back. At the sight of my face, he picked up speed.

"Go!" I screamed into Beaky's back. "Go!"

Beaky didn't need encouragement. He kept the

moped flat out for two more blocks. Then he slowed down a little bit.

I swiveled on my seat. Harry was a half block behind now, and I was beginning to feel safe. As I watched, a vehicle came up behind him and almost hit him when he refused to give up his traffic lane. The vehicle passed under a streetlight. It was a van.

"Keep going," I told Beaky. "Keep it moving."

"He catching us?" Beaky risked a glance over his shoulder.

"No. He won't now. It's the van. Just keep going. They'll pass us, and we can follow them."

They did pass us, not a whole lot later than they had passed Harry. Beaky gave the van a bigger piece of the street than Harry did, but he kept the moped up to speed. He also kept his eyes straight ahead of him.

I didn't. As the van went by, I took a long hard look at it. I couldn't be absolutely certain, but it seemed like the same van all right.

"Don't lose them this time," I told Beaky.

I didn't need to worry. The van went two more blocks, turned a corner, and pulled into a drive beside a cement-block building.

14

Everything would have been perfect if Beaky had only kept his eyes on the road. We could have sped by and gone home to call the cops, telling them exactly where the van was and what the men were doing. But Beaky didn't keep his eyes on the road. Instead, he gawked toward the van, watching the men crawling out of it not twenty feet from where we passed.

The moped hit something. I don't know if it was a pothole, or a rock, or the curb. Whatever it was, it made Beaky jerk on the handlebars. The moped jolted, then flipped.

Beaky screamed. Then he made a series of whimpering cries. I didn't pay much attention. He had his problems; I had mine. I flew off the moped and skidded on my back straight up the driveway. When I stopped skidding, I was still on my back, staring straight up into the faces of the men from the van.

They weren't happy to see us. One of them reached down and dragged me bodily to my feet, while the other one went to check out Beaky.

I was standing there, trying to catch my breath and wondering if any part of me was seriously injured, when the other guy came back, hauling Beaky by one arm.

"I wrecked my jacket," shrieked Beaky as soon as he saw me. "It's brand-new. My mom will kill me."

"What are we going to do about this, Charlie?" asked the man holding Beaky.

"Thank you so much," I said, recovering my wits at last. "We'll just get the moped and go home now. Don't bother about us. We'll be okay."

Charlie didn't answer me. I couldn't see his face too well, but when he spoke, he sounded uncertain. "Let's take them in the building and get a look at them."

At that point, Beaky pulled free and started running. He didn't get far. The man who'd been holding him made a flying tackle, then put Beaky into an arm lock. We were marched into the cement-block building.

As I blinked my eyes in the glare from the bare bulb in the ceiling, I tried not to look around, but I couldn't help it. The inside looked like a big storage shed. It was empty for the most part, except for a few tools and a mass of rectangular objects along a back wall, covered by tarpaulins. I wondered if the objects were refrigerators and televisions.

"I want to go home," whined Beaky.

"Why are you kids following us?" demanded Charlie.

Suddenly I had a brilliant inspiration. "We weren't

following you," I said craftily. "We borrowed a moped and we were trying it out."

"Borrowed?" asked Charlie, his eyes softening.

"You know." I managed a weak smile. "We'll take it back. Honest we will."

Charlie was actually looking pleased when his partner said, "Hey. I saw this kid before!"

"Huh?" Charlie glanced at Beaky.

"It's that ugly girl from the condominiums," said the other guy. "I'll never forget that nose." He stepped closer, peering at Beaky. "And it's no girl either. It's a boy!"

"Are you sure?"

"Yeah, I'm sure. Look at him, Charlie."

But Charlie was too busy looking at me. "And this is his friend," he said softly.

"And they was following us," said his partner.

I ran my eyes around the walls, seeking escape, even though I figured it was impossible. The walls were solid, with only a double garage door, closed, and a small entrance door, also closed. There was one window, about ten feet from me. It was covered by a tattered shade, one corner ripped entirely off, baring glass.

"We won't tell anyone," said Beaky. Both men looked at him, but I looked at the window. Through the uncovered area of glass, I could see a pale blur with dark eyes staring in at us. At first I thought it was a third member of the gang, but then I realized it had to be Harry.

Harry was big and strong and armed with a wrench. He was our only chance. I had to get him inside that building.

I stuck my tongue out at him.

"We can't let them go," said Charlie.

"Then what will we do?" asked the other man.

"We have to—"

There was a pounding on the door. Charlie broke off in midsentence. He glanced rapidly at his partner, then at us, then at the door. The pounding was repeated, louder.

"Cops!" said Charlie.

The door shuddered on its hinges, then burst open. Harry marched in, still grasping his wrench.

He wasn't as large as I'd thought he was. He was wide, covered with bulging muscles and black hair that resembled a bath mat on his naked chest, but he wasn't real tall. He had a horrid ugly pink scar across one shoulder and a little scratch, still seeping blood, on one cheek. He wore untied sneakers and baby blue pajama bottoms and that's all. His eyes were small and dark and vicious.

"What does a man have to do to get any rest?" he demanded.

"We woke you up?" asked Charlie. He sounded horrified.

"Those two punks did." Harry waved his wrench at Beaky and me.

Charlie flicked his eyes at his partner, then quickly back at Harry. His partner edged away from Harry, behind him, toward the wall where the tools were stacked.

"I'm sorry about that," said Charlie, giving a fake smile. "They've been causing us some trouble too, sneaking in here at night and stealing things."

"Not me!" said Beaky.

Charlie's partner picked up a sledgehammer. He slowly raised it over Harry's head.

"Watch out!" I screamed.

Harry stepped neatly to one side and back-armed the man with the wrench.

The man flew halfway across the shed. He hit the cement-block wall about five feet from the floor and slid down into a heap at the bottom. He didn't look as if he would ever move again.

Charlie's eyes grew huge. He backed three steps and lifted both his hands, palms toward Harry, displaying that they were empty.

Harry stepped forward.

"Don't hit me," said Charlie, his voice shaking. "You're big and you have a wrench." He grinned, baring his teeth. "I only have a weak heart."

Harry cocked his head, his small eyes on Charlie.

"Hit him," yelled Beaky, dancing around, keeping clear of the action. "Hit him!"

Harry dropped the wrench. He moved closer to Charlie, his knees slightly bent, his big hands open, extended toward the other man, like a wrestler.

Charlie moved back a few more feet, taking Harry farther from the wrench.

One moment, Charlie's hands were empty. The next, his right one held a knife, its long blade glinting in the light from the bare bulb. He made a quick slashing movement toward Harry.

Harry grinned. His left arm darted out.

Charlie slashed at it.

Harry's right hand grabbed Charlie by the wrist. He lifted his knee and brought Charlie's arm swiftly down across his leg.

There were three sounds in the building. The first was a light clatter of the knife on the cement floor. The second was the sound of a human bone being broken. The third was Charlie's scream.

Harry sat on Charlie's stomach and looked at Beaky and me.

"You're next," he said.

"Me?" I squeaked.

"You busted my window box."

"I saved your life too," I said. I thought that would be safer than mentioning that actually he had broken his own window box.

Harry frowned. Deep inside his solid-looking head, cogs seemed to be turning. I could almost see them move behind the dark eyes.

"We're even," he said.

I hadn't realized I was holding my breath until I heard the sigh of pent-up air being released and felt a pressure ease in my lungs.

"I'll find a telephone," said Beaky. "I'll call the police."

"No cops," said Harry.

"But these men are robbers," said Beaky. "All this stuff in here is stolen. Their van is full of televisions."

I slid my eyes sideways at Beaky. I didn't know whether he was growing more brave or if he was getting dumber. I wouldn't have disagreed with Harry for the world. If Harry said "No cops," then I sure wasn't going to call any cops.

Harry glanced around, his eyes resting briefly on the inert body of Charlie's partner. Then he rolled his eyes toward the ceiling and heaved a deep sigh. "Okay," he said grudgingly. "Call the cops. I guess I wouldn't get any more sleep tonight anyway."

"I'll go with Beaky," I offered quickly. "We'll call the police and come right back, just in case you need anything."

"All I need is a decent night's rest," grumbled Harry. "You kids don't seem to understand that."

I smiled and nodded, following Beaky, my steps quickening as we neared the door.

"Wait a minute!" roared Harry.

"What?" I turned, looking back at Harry, who was squatting comfortably on Charlie.

"Before you call the police, I want one thing straight." He stared hard at Beaky, then at me in turn.

"What's that?" I asked politely.

"You kids want to play cops and robbers in the middle of the night, from now on you pick some other neighborhood. You hear?"

"Yes, sir."

15

Nobody hung any medals on us. As a matter of fact, both Beaky's parents and mine were really irritated with us for sneaking out at night and following the men. They didn't punish us though, so I could say we came out even, except with the kids on the team and at school. They treated both of us with a new respect.

After that, Beaky and I didn't do any more running around in the middle of the night. I can't say I miss it, although I still sometimes wake up around 2:00 A.M. with the feeling I should be somewhere else. Then I think about standing in the rain, and being chased by Harry, and being caught by the men, and I roll over and snuggle down in my soft warm bed and go back to sleep.

I gave Tina her rat for her birthday. She named the rat Fernando, even though I told her it was a girl rat. Tina and Fernando get along real well. I guess they understand each other. However, I have had to delay in getting myself a boy rat, as my mom and Fernando aren't exactly the best of buddies. As a matter of fact, Mom told me that before I ever bring another living creature into our house as a pet, I have to get her permission in writing.

About the only other thing that is new in my life is that I finally gathered up my courage and talked with Coach Bob Baker and Mr. Mathais. I decided that after facing Harry and his wrench, I could face anybody, and I was right. Both Bob Baker and Mr. Mathais were very nice to me. They said they would give me a second chance, but that I was to be very careful that I didn't cause any more trouble.

Our first official baseball game was this afternoon. With the usual luck of Lyttons Union Co-op, we drew Rutledge Rims as our opponents. We all knew they were going to mince us.

They did. I won't even give the final score, as it is too embarrassing.

At the end of the game, the Rutledge guys went over by their bench, and our team came over by ours. Shawn and some of the other players from Lyttons' went into a sort of huddle. I sat on the bench and watched them as I tied one of my shoelaces.

Then Shawn and the other guys broke out of the huddle. They linked arms and they gave our cheer. It was the first I'd heard it. It went:

We are the losers,
But nobody's prouder.
And if you can't hear us,
We'll yell a little louder.

We are the losers,
But nobody's prouder.
And if you can hear us,
Our names are Shawn, Chris, Norris,
Elliot, Ape Ears, and Beaky . . .

Over by the Rutledge bench, Butch put his hands to his ears and waggled them at me.

In the old days, I would have gotten mad over that. Today I only laughed. I put my hands behind my ears and waggled them right back at Butch. Then I gathered up my glove and went to join the rest of my team.

I felt very good, very much in control. I felt as if nobody could mess with me—not even myself.